False
Dandelions

By

Randolph Randy Camp

ISBN: 1478273720
ISBN 13: 9781478273721

Dedicated to the good people of Spotsylvania and Fredericksburg, the place where my dreams were formed.

RANDOLPH CAMP

Table of Contents

Chapter One

Street Dogs

Crawling around at the bottom ain't the life for nobody. Turtle knew that, and Patty knew that. When Turtle shot Patty that night it was more than just two dreams dying. It all began in Washington, DC back in 1990.

On the city's dark side, away from the glorified tour sites, loud rap music fills the late evening air of a decrepit public-housing project. Young kids and teens are hanging out listening and dancing to the music blasting from an opened window. A group of girls rhyme their own song as they play and jump double-dutch under a street lamp. A crew of young boys is standing near a fence that borders the basketball courts. The tallest boy, who looks no more than sixteen, disburses dollar bills to a few of the smaller boys. On the other side of Washington big political deals are made and young politicians dream of making a name for themselves. Here on the Southeast side, drug deals are made and up-and-coming street punks also dream of becoming somebody. The crew of young boys begins to disperse. In the background, night lights illuminate the towering Washington Monument. Breaking away from the group and happily counting his few dollar bills is twelve-year-old Winston Niles. The tallest boy and some of the older boys glance back at young Winston then begin to whisper and giggle among themselves.

"See, told ya' he was stupid," one boy says.

"Yeah, that's why they call 'em Turtle...'cause he's so damn slow an' shit," another boy adds.

All of the boys go their separate ways as they mock and laugh at young Turtle who is very content with his few dollar bills. Turtle climbs the front steps, nearing the door of his apartment. A teenage boy and his girlfriend are cuddled on the steps as young Turtle passes by.

"How much ya' make, Turtle?" the boy asks.

"Five this time!" Turtle excitedly answers.

Shaking their heads in disbelief, the lovebirds simultaneously utter, "Turtle, when ya' ever gonna learn?"

Young Turtle ignores the couple then enters his apartment.

In the living room, Turtle's mother, his two sisters and two brothers are engaged in some type of board game. Boxes of various games: Battleship, Strategy, Payday, Monopoly and Scrabble are stacked near the corner of the large sofa. Through the corner of her eye, Turtle's mother watches him as he tries to sneak by.

"Winston Nelson Niles, now tell me, where was you all evenin'?" Miss Niles asks.

Turtle quickly answers, "Just shootin' some hoops, Mama."

Reading right through his lie, Miss Niles says, "Boy, 'em streets out there can't teach you nuddin'. Why don'tcha com'on over here and join yo' family for a nice game. Betcha these games can teach you more 'bout life than 'em streets out there."

Somewhat reluctantly, young Turtle eases himself down beside his mother as she excitedly rows her dice across the game board.

❧❧

It's twenty years later. On a cool night along Washington's 14th Street, a red '99 Ford Taurus is parked curbside with its hood raised. Turtle, now an old street dog, adjust something on the engine then slams the hood! Inside the car there are shadowy figures of a female in the passenger seat and a young man sitting in the back. Turtle hurries back to the driver-side door. Bursting with frustration, he mouths 'Fuck!' Turtle slides behind the wheel then hastily turns the key in the ignition and rapidly pats the gas pedal. The engine chokes.

"Com'on you piece of shit! Fuck!" Turtle shouts!

Stomping the gas, Turtle tries again. Seconds later, the engine turns. Taking a quick glance at his watch, Turtle sighs, "Shit!"

Provocatively showing a lot skin, sexy Angie sits quietly on the passenger side. She doesn't look a day over twenty but her subtle demeanor is of a worldly woman. Turtle's young protégé Roland, better known as RoRo on the street, sits patiently in the backseat next to a stuffed backpack. Obviously running late to something big, Turtle shifts the gear to 'drive' then floors the gas! The rundown Ford zooms eastward, zigzagging through traffic. A short time later, Turtle pulls the red Taurus into the parking lot of a sleazy motel. Wasting no time, Turtle blindly reach into the backseat. RoRo quickly place the stuffed backpack into Turtle's awaiting hand.

"Keep the car runnin', RoRo. Com'on Angie, I might need you to sweetin' things up wit' these fools," Turtle orders.

Angie shoots Turtle a look then submissively gets out of the car. With the bulging backpack in tow, Turtle fast-steps toward Room 12. As instructed, Angie follows. Turtle knocks on the door, "Yo Preacher, it's me, Turtle."

The door slightly opens. Turtle and Angie slip through the crack in the doorway. Preacher, a smooth-talking drug dealer, and two of his menacing thugs with .38 specials tucked underneath their waistbands, are standing next to the bed topped with a closed briefcase. Angie's tantalizing body is softening the thugs' mean, harden looks.

"You're late, Turtle. Niggas' been shot for lesser things," Preacher says.

Turtle places the stuffed backpack on the bed next to the briefcase then gives Angie a soft shove forward.

Winking at Preacher, Turtle suggests, "How 'bout a lit'l yum-yum for forgiveness?"

Angie tries her best to conceal a dirty look at Turtle. Smartly, Preacher picks up on Angie's feelings.

"Turtle, why ' you disrespectin' the young sistah like that? Come wit' me, sugar. Let me holler at ya' for a minute," Preacher smoothly utters.

Snake-tongued Preacher leads Angie into the adjacent bathroom then shuts the door. Turtle and the two beefy thugs don't move a muscle. All eyes are glued on the briefcase and backpack atop the bed. Inconspicuously, Turtle moves his right hand downward, resting it on the butt of his .44 Magnum tucked under his belt.

In the cramped bathroom, Preacher gives Angie's body a thorough look-over. Angie looks away, trying her best to ignore his scanning eyes.

"Girl, let me school ya' on a few thangs. Hangin' wit' Turtle ain't gonna get ya' nowhere. He thinks small. He lives small. An' he always gonna be small. Yo' sistah, wit' a body like that – and I can already tell you certainly know how to use it – you can have anythang in this world. Just say the word an' we could leave here tonight...together. Girl, Turtle's gotta be pushin' almost thirty-five an' he ain't nuddin' but a runner. It's time for you to roll yo' own dice or you gonna be trapped in his small lit'l world too," Preacher coolly lectures.

Angie has heard these same lines a thousand times from johns, tricks, pimps and wanna-be pimps all over the country. She dealt with them, and she can certainly deal with smooth-tongue Preacher. Angie rolls her eyes then steps toward the door.

"Don'tcha got some business to take care of out there?" Angie coolly asks while turning the doorknob to let herself out.

"Just remember this though, if he ain't goin' nowhere then you ain't goin' nowhere," Preacher nods.

Angie walks out. Preacher steps out concealing his disappointment in luring Angie. Back to business, Preacher signals one of his thugs to check the contents in the swollen backpack. The husky gangster unzips the backpack then turns it upside down. Sandwich bags of crystal meth spill out across the bed.

"Pure ice, baby. None of that dirty Kansas crank shit. Pure Mexican ice," Turtle says.

Preacher and his two sidekicks are satisfied. Preacher gestures Turtle to take the briefcase. Turtle opens it. His eyes widen as he nods his approval.

"And tell yo' boss not to be droppin' shit to me wit' no late motherfuckers no mo' either," Preacher utters.

Turtle ignores Preacher's remarks as he cradles the briefcase then nods to Angie to head out the door. Angie and Turtle leaves the room.

In the parking lot, while walking towards the car, Turtle looks at Angie with a serious expression and asks, "What the fuck Preacher had to say in the bathroom?"

"Nuddin'," Angie quickly answers.

The old Taurus is still running. RoRo gets out of the driver seat then returns to the backseat. Angie slides into the passenger seat as Turtle slips behind the wheel. Turtle blindly hands Roland the briefcase then drives out of the parking lot onto 14th Street. Turtle seems preoccupied. Both Angie and RoRo begin to look at Turtle with puzzled faces as he passes familiar streets, taking them completely out of the usual routine.

Nonchalantly, Turtle continues to drive out of the city towards the I-95 Freeway Junction up ahead. A well-lit road sign alerts...

Exit 32
I-95 South
To Virginia

Concerned, Angie asks, "Where ' we goin', Turtle? You passed the turn. Ain't you droppin' the money off to –"

"That's my money. I ain't nobody's fuckin' errand boy no mo'," Turtle interrupts.

Unlike Angie, RoRo seems content with Turtle's impromptu decision. Turtle turns right onto EXIT 32, heading for a new beginning.

Chapter Two

Welcome to the Country

About a week later, the bright morning sun has awaken bountiful yellow patches of dandelions and other colorful wild flowers in the wide open, backcountry fields of Spotsylvania County, Virginia. The slow-moving Rappahannock River snakes alongside dense woods and acres of vacant farm land then crawls underneath a bridge that joins the sleepy county to the outskirts of Fredericksburg. A few pedestrians, carrying a grocery bag or two, are crossing the old, weathered bridge as vehicles pass them by.

Across the river, at the edge of the city, a towering billboard advertises 'SERV CITY TRUCKSTOP.'

Nearby, an Interstate 95off-ramp supplies the busy truck stop with a steady flow of road-weary truckers and travelers in need of a break from the bustling highway. Back across the bridge, a Spotsylvania County school bus carrying a full load of high school students is making its way on a two-lane blacktop lined with sporadic open fields and quite a few vacant country homes accessorized with roadside mailboxes. Weathered 'FOR SALE' signs are posted in numerous fields and on the many unkept lawns of empty homes. The real estate fallout of 2008 and 2009 has taken its toll on Spotsylvania County, but there are a few who've managed to keep their heads above water. As the busload of students continue along the blacktop, some gaze out the window at a man spraying weed-killer on numerous dandelions sprouting on his otherwise well-manicured lawn. A short distance down the road, a local furniture store delivery truck and a flashy new Cadillac Escalade are parked in the front yard of a modest house, a house in which Turtle has chosen to start anew. Delivery workers are unloading the truck and carrying high-quality tables, beds, dressers, sofas and chairs into the house.

In the kitchen of their new hideaway, leaning against the sink, Turtle and Angie are enthralled in a juicy kiss. In partial view of delivery workers angling a sofa and loveseat through the front door, Angie is being somewhat coy as she tries to block Turtle's right hand from cupping her breast.

"Turtle, stop. The delivery guys," Angie says.

"Hm, after I get mines then they can come in here an' get theirs," Turtle utters.

Angie's succulent lips and soft bedroom eyes can control any man, but Turtle, undoubtedly, is the one making the rules here.

"Baby, you know I don't run like that no mo'. You promised, remember? My debt is paid, right?" Angie asks.

Turtle steps away from Angie. Slyly, he tries to avoid her questions.

"Hey, I was just playin' wit' ya Angie. No mo' runnin'. Ain't nobody gonna be lookin' for us in the sticks. Hey, we got cash. We ' safe an' we turnin' a new leaf now, baby. No mo' DC shit. Can't nobody tell me shit now. 'Em days is dead," Turtle preaches.

With a bit of concern, Angie replies, "That was a lot of paper we took Turtle. Those DC dogs just don't play like that. Are you sure 'bout this country thing?"

"Baby, you be stressin' too much. Relax. I got this. This lit'l stick town gonna be mines in no time. Soon as RoRo get back from his fact-finding mission at the school then I can start my thang an' you can do yo' thang. See baby, I got it all under control. I got this. Nice an' smooth. So relax, sweet thang," Turtle explains.

Turtle inches toward Angie, lowering his lips to her left breast. Angie pulls down her low-cut blouse to expose her left nipple to Turtle's awaiting lips.

❀❀

The traveling school bus is now parked along the shoulder of the blacktop next to a vast field of wild flowers. Miss Taylor leads her horticulture students through a sea of colorful weeds and wild flowers then stops in the middle of a patch of dandelions in various stages of growth. The dense dandelion patch consist of fully blossomed, bright yellow flower heads and countless white cotton-like lollipop heads of tiny, seed-bearing parachutes ready to take flight at the slightest breeze. RoRo, or Roland as his teacher and new classmates calls him, is acting peculiar. The city-cool new student is quietly easing in the background of a group of predominantly white, country-raised teenagers. Sneakily, RoRo eavesdrops on his classmates' private conversations and inconspicuously observes everything and everybody around him.

Miss Taylor glances at the long-stemmed, yellow flowers around her then snaps off two plants at the lower stem. The two plants look extremely similar from a distance. Holding one stemmed plant in her right hand and the other in her left hand, Miss Taylor is poised to give her students a pop quiz.

Raising her right hand, Miss Taylor asks, "What's the common name of this plant?"

Without hesitation, the entire group answers in unison, "Dandelion."

"Good," Miss Taylor says while raising her left hand, "And the name of this plant?"

Again, instantly, the whole class responds collectively, "Dandelion."

"Not exactly," Miss Taylor says.

Glancing at one another, the students are puzzled.

Continuing, Miss Taylor elaborates, "Notice how the plant in my left hand is taller and has multiple forked stems carrying flower heads on each stem, and the one in my right hand only has one straight stem. This one in my left hand is known as a false dandelion. Notice how this false dandelion stem is solid, unlike the one in my right hand, which is hollow. The yellow flower heads may look the same but there are distinct differences between the two. False dandelions are much more difficult to get rid of due to their tougher stems and roots.

Some of the students are momentarily distracted and begin to turn their heads toward the parked bus. Miss Taylor continues to lecture but coolly watches the activity near the school bus through the corner of her eye. Exiting the bus is Jesse Raine and LaBrea Woods. Sweethearts since last summer, the interracial couple has raised a few eyebrows around the county. Jesse stands tall wearing a confident, big country boy smile. LaBrea's flawless brown skin and curvaceous body, wrapped tightly in stylish jeans, turns all the guys' heads. RoRo, the new kid, can't keep his eyes off of LaBrea's swaying hips as she and Jesse walks across the field.

"Damn!" RoRo utters.

"Roland, we don't speak that way in my class. And I hope you get that enthused about plants and horticulture as you do about LaBrea's figure," Miss Taylor quips with a sigh.

Amused by their teacher's remarks, the rest of the students enjoy a light chuckle. LaBrea blushes while Jesse, on the other hand, nonchalantly continues to don his cowboy smile.

RoRo definitely stands out from his new classmates. There's nothing country about him. His harden face says that he's had a lot of experience in his young, urban years.

Miss Taylor shoots Jesse and LaBrea a scornful look as they join the group.

"Since you two felt it wasn't important to join us earlier, maybe you two already know this stuff. What can you two tell us about dandelions?" Miss Taylor asks the two lovebirds.

LaBrea bends over to pluck a white, lollipop head of tiny, weightless spheres then playfully blows them off of the flower head. The air around LaBrea is suddenly filled with a white cloud of floating dandelion spheres.

"I like making a wish every time I see those little cute parachute things blowing in the wind," LaBrea says with a gleeful smile.

"Those are the airborne seeds which some people do refer to as dandelion wishes. Hopefully these seeds will find fertile soil and take root," Miss Taylor explains while turning to Jesse with a knowing nod, "Got something to add, Jesse?"

"People put 'em in salads. Even make wine from 'em too," Jesse adds.

Street-wise RoRo raises his eyebrow, "Wine? Dandelion wine?"

Miss Taylor interjects, "Jesse, make sure you tell Ma'Raine I said hello, alright?"

Jesse nods 'okay' as Miss Taylor continues, "Class, the common dandelion is a tricky flower. And the false dandelion is even trickier. At first they do seem so appealing to us with that bountiful beautiful head of bright yellow petals, and yes they do have some good culinary benefits as Jesse had pointed out, but we spend a lot of time and money trying to get rid of these dandelions 'cause they invade our lawns and steal the nutrients in the soil. They invade and suffocate the roots of grass and other plants. They just take over."

Miss Taylor steps away to focus on another wild flower. The students follow her lead. RoRo shifts his eyes on LaBrea's curvy backside as Jesse's white hand gently slides into her back pocket. RoRo turns up his upper lip in a mixture of distaste and obvious jealousy.

Chapter Three

Dandelion Wine

Jesse's grandmother, Ma'Raine, is well known in Spotsylvania County. She's been supplying folks around here with her homemade wine for years. Loud country music echoes out of a Dodge pickup leaving Ma'Raine's dusty driveway then hurriedly speeds away down the two-lane blacktop.

A Spotsylvania County Sheriff patrol cruiser turns off of the blacktop then parks in front of the shabby house with a leaning, screened porch and half-rotted wooden steps. The Sheriff steps out of the cruiser. Wearing a cheerful grin on his country brown face, Sheriff Woods walks across the neglected yard towards the leaning porch.

"Ma'Raine? Ma'Raine?" the Sheriff calls.

The battered porch screen door opens wider. Frazzled-haired Ma'Raine appears in the doorway. The bright sunlight hits her pale face. She blocks the sun with her right hand.

"C'mon in, Woody. Da' sun's hurtin' my eyes," Ma'Raine greets. Sheriff Woods carefully climbs the rotten steps as Ma'Raine holds the screen door open for him. The spacious porch is ornamented with aging patio furniture.

"Have a seat Woody an' tell me what's new," Ma'Raine cordially says as she sits.

Flashing that big friendly grin of his, the Sheriff plants himself comfortably next to Ma'Raine.

"Just came to arrest you again for violation of Virginia Alcohol Beverage Control Code Title Four Point One, illegal sale of alcohol without a license. Just doing my job, Ma'Raine. Just doing my job," Sheriff Woods says while giving Ma'Raine a playful wink.

"Aw, you an' yo' silly codes. Don't worry none, Woody. I got yo' bottles already sittin' in da' back. Now tell me whatcha really came here for," Ma'Raine utters with a touch of seriousness.

"You got new neighbors just down the road a ways," the Sheriff says.

"They good people?" Ma'Raine asks.

"Don't know yet. Time will tell. Sometimes people ain't always who they say they are. Time will tell though," Sheriff Woods answers in his wise Southern drawl.

"Aw, Woody, people ' just kinda like 'em dande-lions, just blowin' in da' wind tryin' to find a place to call home," Ma'Raine utters.

Glancing at his watch, Sheriff Woods stands, "I better get on now. Don't wanna scare yo' customers off with my patrol car sittin' out front."

"By the way, Woody, how's yo' boy Lamar doin'? That's a shame how he came back from the war all mangled up like that," Ma'Raine says with sincere eyes.

"He still goes to physical therapy an' he just loves 'em new crutches the VA in Richmond gave him. Still gotta ways to go yet but he's adjusting. Matter ' fact, now he's tryin' to get some kinda loan," shrug-ging his shoulders, Sheriff Woods continues, "Last night he told me how the local news and the paper done made him out to be some type of hero but he said he just don't feel like one."

"Well God bless him. If I had an extra leg I'd give it to 'em in a minute," Ma'Raine says then continues as she stands, "I betta go inside an' get yo' bottles 'fo ya put me in one of 'em handcuffs an' haul me off to jail."

Ma'Raine disappears in the house as the Sheriff patiently waits on the porch. Moments later, Ma'Raine returns with two quart-size bottles gener-ically labeled MA'RAINE'S DANDELION WINE. She hands the bottles to the happily grinning Sheriff.

"All charges and alcohol beverage code viola-tions have been cordially dropped," Sheriff Woods quips.

"Aw, you an' yo' silly codes," Ma'Raine sighs.

Sheriff Woods gives Ma'Raine a tender kiss on her cheek then teases, "I'll be back to arrest you in a couple ' weeks."

"Yo' bottles ' be waitin' fo' ya," Ma'Raine nods with a loving smile. Sheriff Woods exits the porch.

Chapter Four

Lamar

A taxi pulls up curbside in front of the Fredericksburg Savings Bank. Equipped with his custom-made forearm crutches, young Iraq war vet Lamar Woods hands the cabbie several crumbled bills for the fare as the rear door opens. Lamar struggles to scoot out but gestures to the driver that he can manage on his own. The cabbie nods 'okay.'

The taxi pulls away. Keeping balance on his customized crutches by using his good right leg, Lamar slowly steps toward the bank entrance door as his paralyzed left leg dangles freely. Lamar is unaware of the curious faces peering out of the bank window.

Some customers stare as Lamar enters the bank. Maneuvering his aluminum crutches, Lamar heads straight toward the LOAN MANAGER'S DESK.

A vase of fresh-cut, yellow-petal dandelions and a gold-lettered name plate spelling JENNIFER DAY ornament the desk. Only a year or two older than Lamar, youthful-looking Jennifer tries her best to be professional as possible and not stare as Lamar leans his crutches against the cushion chair next to the desk then sits.

"What can I do for you today?" Jennifer asks.

As the young vet struggles to speak, it becomes apparent that Lamar's left leg wasn't the only part of his body damaged in the war, "I wanna..gg..get a bus so I ca..can st..st..start me a..um..um..a shut.. shuttle business."

Jennifer's face contorts from being both amused and confused as she eyes the custom-made forearm crutches propped against the chair.

"Who will be driving the shuttle bus?" Jennifer asks.

"Mm..me," Lamar quickly answers.

Jennifer is impressed with Lamar's focus and apparent desire but is still curious on certain issues. Jennifer asks, "Don't you need a special CDL, a commercial license to drive a bus?"

Filled with a mixture of strong ambition and a dab of naivety, Lamar answers, "Aft..after I gg..get the mm..money fr..from the loan then I ca..can gg.. get me a bb..bus an' license. See, po' people in the cc..country like Spotsy' ania cc..can't 'fford to pay fo' a cab all the tt..time wwh..when they gotta come here to Fred'burg tt..to shop an' stuff."

Moved by Lamar's genuine compassion and determined spirit, Jennifer retrieves a loan application form from the bottom drawer.

"We're going to start things with our loan application. Just a few simple questions," Jennifer says.

"Oo..okay," Lamar nods.

With pen in hand, Jennifer is ready for Lamar's answers. Jennifer asks, "Name?"

"La..Lamar Wo..Woods," he quickly answers.

Jennifer writes then asks, "Age?"

"Tw..twenty-two," Lamar says.

"How much of a loan are you applying for? Five hundred dollars? Two thousand dollars? Ten thousand?" Jennifer questions.

"Umm..Ummm..How much a bb..bus cost?" Lamar asks.

Amused by Lamar's innocence, Jennifer smiles then scribbles something on the application form.

"Occupation?" Jennifer continues.

Lamar ponders then explains, "Nnn..now I just wa..wait ff..for my dis..disabil..disability ch..check bb..but I ww..was a dd..demo spec in the army 'fo I gg..got hurt."

Putting the pieces together in her head as she digests Lamar's words, Jennifer illuminates as she realizes that this is the young Iraq war veteran who was featured in the local press recently. Suddenly, an idea comes over Jennifer. She shoves the application form aside then looks Lamar directly into his eyes. Suspiciously, Jennifer lowers her voice as she leans closer to Lamar, "Mister Woods, it's going to take a few days to process your application. We should know by early next week if I can help you or not."

Lamar digs out his cellphone from his shirt pocket then reaches for his crutches.

"Th..thank you, Miss Da..Day," Lamar nods.

"Call me Jennifer or just Jenny if you like. I can call a taxi for you," Jennifer offers.

Lamar tucks his cellphone away then struggles to stand.

"Oo..okay an' you cc..can jj..just cc..call me Lamar," he says.

Using her desk phone, Jennifer calls a cab while several bank customers stare at Lamar slowly making his way towards the door. Jennifer retrieves her purse from the floor. She sneakily glances at her coworkers, ensuring that no one is watching her. Suspiciously, Jennifer folds Lamar's loan application then shoves it into her purse.

Chapter Five

Turtlenopoly Baby!

Miss Taylor's horticulture class is returning back to school from their field trip. LaBrea and Jesse are sitting snugly close near the middle of the slow-moving bus. The way Jesse looks at LaBrea there's no doubt that this is true love. LaBrea finger-brushes Jesse's hair as he gazes into her eyes.

Seated strategically behind the love birds is the snooping new kid RoRo. With his ears and shifty eyes inconspicuously aimed at Jesse and LaBrea, RoRo listens to every word uttered and unapologetically observes their intimacy.

"You wanna help me pick dandelions Saturday for Grandma?" Jesse asks.

"Imagine that, the next Johnny Cash pickin' flowers to make bootleg wine," LaBrea teases.

Jesse tries to steal a kiss but LaBrea playfully shifts her face away.

"Grandma got a lot of orders to fill," Jesse pleads.

"I swear, all you guys are the same. Y'all would say just 'bout anything to get a girl all alone in some faraway flower field so you can have yo' way with her," LaBrea quips.

With perfect timing, Jesse takes advantage of LaBrea's playfulness and quickly plants a soft, wet kiss on her unsuspecting lips!

Enchanted by the kiss, LaBrea immediately utters, "What time Saturday should I meet you at Ma'Raine's?"

Quietly taking it all in, RoRo inconspicuously nods his head as the bus comes to a crawl and enters the school entranceway.

Minutes later, Miss Taylor and her students are exiting the bus. As always, Jesse and LaBrea are holding hands. RoRo taps Jesse on his shoulder as they head back inside the school.

"Yo Jesse, can I holler at ya' for a minute?" RoRo asks.

Jesse gestures LaBrea to go on without him. LaBrea ignores her boyfriend's suggestion and waits for him just mere inches away. Jesse and RoRo step aside along the sidewalk as their classmates pass by.

"Yo dude, you seem pretty educated about them weeds an' flowers an' shit out there. Can people really make liquor from 'em dandelions?" RoRo asks.

While awaiting Jesse's response, RoRo's eyes slyly shift to LaBrea's shapely butt squeezed in and perfectly rounding out her tight jeans.

Unaware of RoRo's roaming eyes, Jesse cordially responds, "I tell ya' what, Roland –"

Offering a halfhearted fist-bump, RoRo interjects, "Call me RoRo."

Continuing, Jesse says, "Alright, RoRo, just between you an' me, I'll bring you a sample of my Grandma's stuff on Monday. Best dandelion wine 'round here!"

"Cool. Thanks dude," RoRo nods with a shifty eye.

LaBrea steps closer to Jesse. She grabs his hand and leads him away from RoRo.

"Jesse, I don't like him. There's something about him," LaBrea utters.

"He's new here. Give the guy a chance," Jesse suggests.

Still standing in the grass along the sidewalk, RoRo can't seem to take his eyes off of LaBrea's backside as she and Jesse enter the school.

☙❧

On a cool, breezy evening, Jesse's mother Patty Raine anxiously awaits her fate as she hastily goes through a small pile of lottery scratch-offs at the kitchen table. A bottle of MA'RAINE'S DANDELION WINE and two empty glasses are centered on the table. A plentiful plate of baked ham, mashed potatoes and seasoned greens sits across from Patty. She sighs in disappointment then shoves the losing scratch-offs aside.

"Jesse, your supper's getting' cold!" Patty yells.

Down the hall, Jesse's bedroom is filled with twangy music from his acoustic guitar. Colorful posters of country music legends Willie Nelson and Johnny Cash grace the walls. An 8X10 framed photo of Jesse and LaBrea is perched atop the nightstand. Sitting on the edge of his bed picking and strumming his big-ticket guitar, Jesse ignores his mother's call, "Jesse! Supper!"

Constructing a new song, Jesse abruptly stop strumming then jot down lyrics on a blank sheet of paper beside him.

"Jesse!" his mother yells from the kitchen again.

Jesse puts his guitar aside then springs up. He answers, "Comin'!"

Jesse eases behind his mom still seated at the table. He begins to massage her neck and shoulders then plants a tender kiss on her cheek.

"Sit down and eat," Patty says while reaching for an empty glass.

Jesse glances at the small pile of losing scratch-offs atop the table then sits. Patty pours herself a taste of her mother's homemade wine. Cutting the meat on his plate, Jesse reassuringly says, "Mama, if the lottery don't get us outta here my songs will."

Patty ponders then sips her wine. She shakes her head in frustration.

"Ya ' know, Jesse. I'm just stuck here. Stuck. Yo' daddy used to say 'the only thing ever leavin' this damn place is that muddy water in the Rappahannock'," Patty utters.

Jesse attempts to change the subject, "Grandma wants me to help her this weekend."

The mentioning of her mother rubs Patty the wrong way. She stands then softly mumbles as she steps away from the table, "Some things just ain't worth repairing. I gotta get ready for work."

For years Jesse has been the buffer between his mom and his grandmother. He never gives up on a future reunion, "Mama, why you –"

Patty quickly interrupts, "Jesse, not all women is meant to be mothers. Ma'Raine might be a good grandma to you but she was never a mother to me."

There's a brief silence as Patty grins then awkwardly blurts, "But that ol' bitch makes the best damn dandelion wine in Spotsylvania County though."

Patty leaves the kitchen while Jesse continues to finish his plate.

A short time later, Jesse's at the sink washing dishes. Wearing a sexy, revealing black dress, Patty quietly sneaks across the kitchen. With his back turned, Jesse's totally unaware of his mother's brief presence as she discreetly leaves out the living room door. Outside, Patty passes a late model, blue Chevy Nova then quickly slides into her green Toyota Camry parked in the driveway.

Meanwhile, back inside, Jesse drains the dirty sink water then walks out of the kitchen towards the hallway. Thinking that his mom's getting dressed for work, Jesse stands near her bedroom door. The door is slightly ajar.

Jesse makes small talk while he waits, "Mama, did I tell ya' we gotta new student at school? Seems like a nice guy. LaBrea don't like him already though."

There's no response. Jesse is puzzled. The hallway light illuminates Patty's bedroom as Jesse shoves the door open. Jesse is surprised to find his mother's waitress uniform still laid out across her bed. Baffled, Jesse dash down the hallway towards the bathroom and calls out, "Mama? Mama?"

ⓒⓞ

Down the road, the newcomers have settled into their country nest. In the living room, Angie and RoRo are sitting around the coffee table listening to Turtle's takeover plans. Turtle's .44 Magnum, his two tall cans of beer and a set of car keys rest atop the coffee table.

In spite of his elementary education and sometimes uncontrollable consumption of alcohol, Turtle tries his best to articulate himself as a leader. A little woozy, Turtle periodically slurs his words as he breakdown his strategy to his young clan, "Did ya' see all 'em 'For Sale' signs around here? I ain't no Donald Trump but there's one thing I did learn from playin' that monopoly game when I was growin' up in the projects an' that's ya gotta buy up all the fuckin' real estate and property you can if ya' wanna be in control an' win. Just watch me. This town's gonna be turtlenopolized real fast! All that dirty paper gonna get cleaned when I buy this place up. Just watch me! Turtlenopoly baby!"

"What if nobody wanna sell to you?" Angie asks.

Quite sure of himself, Turtle quickly answers, "Paper. Big paper. Benjamins. Lots of benjamins." Giving Angie a knowing wink, Turtle continues, "And wherever there's truckers there's got to be lot lizards and plenty of ho's. And I know somebody's cuttin' in on the action. Angie, you know what to do. See who's runnin' the show over at Serv City."

Angie nods okay as RoRo interjects, "Believe it or not, homemade dandelion wine could be our new dope. The shit's almost legal 'round here and it's fuckin' everywhere, even in our front yard an' all these country motherfuckers be drinkin' that shit!"

Puzzled, Angie glances at Turtle. Simultaneously, Turtle and Angie looks at RoRo like he's crazy.

"Dandelion wine?" Turtle asks.

RoRo explains, "Yo, I'm serious. This dude's grandmother got –"

"RoRo, you only been here a hot minute an' you already gone country," Angie quips while shaking her head in disbelief then grabbing the keys off the coffee table. She stands and heads for the door, "I'm outta here. Me an' the new caddy's goin' for a ride."

RoRo's enthusiasm has gotten Turtle's attention. Taking large gulps of his beer, Turtle inches closer to his young protege as RoRo excitedly shares his new-found knowledge of the local bootleg wine business.

"Yeah man, this white dude at school supposed to be bringin' me a sample of his grandma's shit an' we can easily cut in on their hustle," RoRo proclaims.

Draining his second can of beer, Turtle burps then drunkenly adds, "Not just cut in but take over that shit. RoRo, you been wit' me for a long time. Remember when you ran away an' I got yo' ass outta that teen homeless shelter? Ya' been my boy ever since, dog. You're a true dog, RoRo. And when I take this lit'l country ass town you ' gonna be like my vice president or some shit like that."

Barely able to sit up straight, Turtle offers a weak fist-bump to RoRo. With no other adult in his some-what aimless life, young Roland has grown to enjoy these periodic, brotherly moments as his small fist meets Turtle's halfway.

Chapter Six

Serv City

Sparkling moonlight flickers from the shiny spinning rims of the lustrous Cadillac Escalade moving across the bridge. Sitting pretty behind the wheel, Angie's in full control, which is something she's not allowed to be in Turtle's presence. Across the river, bright spotlights illuminate the massive Serv City Truckstop.

Countless rows of parked tractor-trailers fill the side and rear parking lots of the vast truck stop. Scantily dressed ladies, footed in three-inch heels, slither through the narrow walkways in between the closely parked eighteen-wheelers. A trucker pokes his head out of his cab. His eyes follow the enticing swagger of a passing lot lizard.

"Lord have mercy! Help me Jesus! Mmmm, mama!" the trucker says with hunger eyes.

"If ya' like it, come an' get it," the lady flirts.

Across the street from the sizeable gas mart and adjoining restaurant is the two-story Serv City Inn, providing lodging for the weary travelers and a quick bed for the numerous lot lizards and prostitutes servicing the lonely truckers.

A '77 Chevy Nova pulls up in front of the restaurant's big, clear window.

Jesse steps out of his muscled Nova with his mother's waitress uniform draped over his left forearm. Through the window, two waitresses glance at Jesse then hurriedly whisper something to each other.

The dining room is near full capacity. Chatter fills the air as Jesse enters. He looks around for his mother Patty. No Patty. Puzzled, Jesse walks toward the two waitresses with his mother's uniform dangling from his arm. A bus boy clearing a nearby table notices Jesse. Speaking with a thick drawl, the young bus boy tries to steal Jesse's attention, "Hey Jesse, 'been writin' any new songs? I just bought my first guitar!"

Preoccupied with other matters at the moment, Jesse ignores his enthusiastic young fan. Jesse approaches the waitresses.

"Ain't my Mama workin' tonight? She forgot her uniform," Jesse utters with a curious expression.

Concealing the truth, the two waitresses awkwardly shrug their shoulders. Then, innocently, one of the waitresses starts to spill the beans, "She might be in –"

"I think Patty's off tonight," the other waitress smartly injects.

Lenny, the burly restaurant manager, appears behind Jesse.

"Jesse, yo' mama ain't working tonight," Lenny says.

Jesse turns around to face Lenny, "Ya know where she's at then?"

Evasively, Lenny dodges Jesse's question by suddenly turning to his waitresses standing nearby.

"Don't y'all have work to do? Com'on now, we gotta packed house," Lenny says with a touch of bass in his voice.

The two waitresses scatter away. Reluctantly, Jesse turns around to exit the bustling diner. Abruptly, Jesse's face lights up as he looks out the big window pane and sees a green Toyota Camry in the parking lot of the Serv City Inn across the street. With his mother's waitress uniform swinging on his arm, Jesse dash out the door! Hastily, thick-neck Lenny digs his cell phone out of his shirt pocket.

"Carl, a heads up. Patty's boy just spotted her car. He's on his way," Lenny alarms his brother then tucks his phone away.

Fast-stepping to the parking lot, Jesse quickly tosses his mother's uniform into his Nova then hurries across the street to the Serv City Inn.

Behind the closed door of room 103, the lights are dimly lit. Several cottage cheese containers rest atop the nightstands. In the darkish, shadowy room, the sound of licking, slurping and the moaning sound of a man enjoying his meal fills the air. Spread out across the bed covered with nothing but a thin layer of cottage cheese, Jesse's mother Patty shuts her eyes in shame as a naked, hairy man happily begins to lick up the patch of cottage cheese between her thighs.

"Mmmm..Mmmmm..Mmm, you gotta goooood cottage cheese pussy," the man says while working his tongue.

Patty lies motionless as the hairy man slowly works his way up along her belly then up to the cottage cheese coating her buxom breasts.

"Mmmmm…Mmmm, goooood fuckin' tits… Mmmmm," the man continues.

Meanwhile, outside in the parking lot, a curvaceous lot lizard laced in a skimpy g-string bikini and three-inch stilettos flirts and leads a horny-eyed trucker towards the Inn's side entrance.

Only a few feet away, Jesse totally ignores the dubious activity in front of him. He's too concerned about his mother's whereabouts right now. Jesse heads straight toward the Inn's main entrance and enters the lobby.

Jesse is immediately greeted by Carl, the Inn's manager and fat-head brother of big Lenny. Purposely, Carl blocks Jesse's path and tries to stall him.

"Ain't you the local star 'round here? People be talkin' 'bout 'em songs you be singin'. They say you a pretty good picker on that guitar too. I tell ya' what, let me take you to our lounge," Carl says while throwing his arm over Jesse's shoulder and taking a few steps across the lobby towards a corridor leading into a spacious lounge. Although his ears are locked on each and every word from Carl's mouth, on the surface it seems as though Jesse isn't at all interested in Carl's tour as he steadily turns his head in every direction looking for his mother. Continuing, Carl elaborates about the lounge, "This is where we bring in bands from outta town and we gotta big talent show comin' up too so kids like yo'self there can get some –"

Jesse interjects, "Look, I seen my Mama's car out front. You know where sh —"

Jesse is interrupted by a familiar loud voice coming from the hallway across the lobby. Although he's unable to see her, Jesse can detect his mother's voice a mile away as she yells, "Damn it, Carl! Didn't I tell y'all to put more fuckin' towels in room one-o-three?!"

Across the lobby, down the hall and still out of view from Carl and Jesse, Patty's head protrudes from room 103. She's totally naked with bits of cottage cheese in her hair and dried pieces of it glued to her face. Pissed off, Patty slams the door shut!

Seconds later, Jesse stands in front of room 103 wearing a baffled face. A few steps behind him, Carl mouths 'Oh shit!'

Jesse knocks on the door. Thinking it's the maid, Patty loudly yells, "About fuckin' time y'all got my fuckin' towels!"

The door swings open. With her face covered with cottage cheese and draped in a bed sheet, Patty stands frozen in complete surprise. Equally stunned, Jesse sees the naked, hairy man sitting on the edge of the bed reaching for his wallet next to empty cottage cheese containers atop the nearby nightstand. There's a long moment of silence then Jesse abruptly just walks away in utter shock.

Ashamed, Patty desperately calls out to her son, "Jesse! Jesse! ...Shit! I hate this fuckin' place! This fuckin' life!..Jesse! Jesse!"

Jesse doesn't look back. With his head hung in disappointment, he walks slowly back towards the lobby area where fat Carl is standing. Carl looks as if he wants to say something to Jesse to pick his spirit up but nothing surfaces. Then, awkwardly, Carl suddenly spurts, "Son, ain't too many people can make five hundred big ones for an hour's work. Yo' mama's just doin' what she needs to do, that's all."

To Carl's surprise, Jesse stops and turns around.

"Any prize money in that talent show you was talkin' about?" Jesse calmly asks.

"Sho' nuf. Eight hundred big ones for the winner," Carl answers.

Jesse nods then asks, "When's the –"

"Be here in two weeks," Carl quickly injects.

Jesse nods 'thanks' to Carl then sighs as he walks out knowing that things between his mother and him will never be the same from this point on.

Outside in the parking lot, Jesse's '77 Nova leaves as Angie arrives behind the wheel of Turtle's new flashy Cadillac Escalade. Angie parks in front of the restaurant. Peering out the big window pane, a group of men begin to stare at the Escalade's eye-catching, sparkling rims. As Angie steps down out of the tall Escalade, boyish cat calls fill the air as passing truckers turn their heads with gazing eyes. Seemingly, every man in the parking lot is leering at Angie's super-model good looks and her tantalizing coke-bottle curves as she walks toward the entrance door.

The restaurant is packed weary travelers and hungry truckers. Angie enters with horny eyes following her every move. The air is filled with constant chatter. A waitress approaches Angie with a sunny, mile-long smile.

"We're really hopping tonight but if you follow me I think we gotta clean table 'round the corner," the waitress says with honest Southern charm.

"Actually, I didn't come here to eat. Who do I talk to 'bout getting a job?" Angie asks.

"Waitress? We certainly could use some help," the perky waitress says.

"Maybe...or other things," Angie coolly answers.

The waitress sees Lenny standing near the register giving a handful of rolled coins to the cashier. She makes eye contact and signals Lenny to come over.

"That's the manager. He's the one to talk to," the waitress utters.

With his eyes focusing on Angie, Lenny approaches.

"Is there a problem?" Lenny asks.

"She's looking for a job," the energetic waitress quickly answers while stepping away.

"I'm Lenny. We can talk in my office. Com'on," Lenny says while trying like hell to keep his eyes off of Angie's enticing curves. He leads Angie across the bustling floor to his office just behind the cash register area.

Aside from the employee work schedule, the walls of Lenny's office are covered with posters of busty, nearly nude ladies standing alongside customized motorcycles and classic muscles cars. His desk is a mess with clustered invoices, old receipts and order tickets. Angie sits across the desk coolly studying Lenny's leering eyes behind his pretentious demeanor.

"So what's yo' name?" Lenny asks.

Fully aware of what her curves do to men like Lenny, Angie conducts herself as a confident woman twice her age. She coolly answers, "I go by Angie."

"You from 'round here or you ride a bicycle?" Lenny continues.

Baffled, Angie cringes, "What?"

Lenny elaborates, "You must not be from 'round here then. That's that ol' country folk talk when they see people they ain't used to seein'...You ever been a wait—"

Angie interrupts, "Look, I ain't in yo' office to bullshit. I maybe young but I've been around. You got people passing through here an' they gotta eat, they gotta sleep, an' sometimes they may need a lit'l pleasure. And we both know that somebody gotta service all ' those needs."

Lenny is blown away by Angie's frankness. Immediately, he digs out his cellphone from his shirt pocket and calls his brother.

"Get yo' ass over here right now! I got somebody sittin' here in my office you gotta meet!" Lenny excitedly tells Carl.

Tucking his phone away, Lenny is trying his best to keep his eyes off of Angie's buxom chest as he breakdown the shady side of Serv City, "My brother Carl runs the hotel 'cross the street and control all the action in the truckers' lot. The girls get a percentage of what they bring in. An' every now an' then we get 'em crazies wit' 'em wild fetishes an' Carl lets the girls keep all ' that money for themselves."

Angie calmly nods as Lenny continues, "Well, I'm gonna get on back out there an' you just wait right here for Carl."

Chapter Seven

Doing Laundry

The following day, Turtle's flashy-rimmed Escalade turns off of single-lane Route 227 into the graveled lot ON SPOT REALTY. The crunchy sound of the moving gravel is music to Agent Danny Stone's ears as he peers through the blinds. As the tumbling housing and real estate market continually take a dive all across the country, rural Spotsylvania County has been hit especially hard. Turtle's been ON SPOT REALTY's only client in quite some time and he's certainly a welcoming sight for Danny's sore eyes. Turtle parks his elegant Escalade next to Danny's Ford Escort and steps out toting a leather attaché case.

Excitedly, Danny opens the door with a hearty handshake, "Hey there Mister Turtle! Everything's alright wit' the house I hope."

"Everything's cool Danny my man," Turtle says while stepping into the colorful flyer-covered office. Every inch of wall space is plastered with numerous pictures and various sized advertisements of vacant lots, houses, open fields and dilapidated farms throughout Spotsylvania County.

"What can I do ya' for t'day, Mister Turtle? Oh, an' befo' I forget, I got 'em house papers an' deed for ya' to sign too," Danny utters.

With a tight grip on his fancy attaché case, Turtle goes to the left wall and begins to scan the colorful 'For Sale' flyers of land and properties.

"Danny my man, I need another favor. I appreciate how you got me into that house so fast with no questions asked and now I need to clean some mo' dough," Turtle says while studying the flyers.

"How much we ' talkin' 'bout here?" Danny asks.

Turtle turns around, walks over to Danny's desk and calmly opens his attaché case. Danny takes a glance at the rows of neatly bundled hundred-dollar bills and begins to nod with a pleasing grin.

"See, that's why I like you, Danny my man. You don't ask questions. You just do what you do. I like that! Everybody should be like that!" Turtle proclaims.

"Hell, I don't give a shit where ya' come from or if ya' wanna be called Mister Squirrel, Mister Possum or Mister Rabbit, just as long as ya' got some'em that everybody understands then ya' gonna be alright wit' me," Danny explains.

As Turtle closes the attaché case, Danny's face lights up.

"I got the perfect seller for ya' Mister Turtle! Ol' Bobby Lewis ' been trying to sell his farm for three years now. Gotta lotta acres on it too," Danny says while eying Turtle's shiny shoes and stylish trousers.

"Some'em wrong, my man?" Turtle asks.

"Ol' Bobby Lewis is pure country through an' through. If we go see Ol' Bobby an' he sees that you ain't gotta bit of country in ya' at all, especially wit' 'em city-slick shoes an' 'em city-slick pants on, well, he might not be so willin' to part wit' that ol' farm. Ol' Bobby wanna keep things country, that's all. I think he'll swallow it better if we get ya' countrified a bit," Danny explains.

"Countrified?" Turtle asks.

"Yup. Countrified. Befo' we go out an' see Mister Lewis we can swing into town an' get ya' some denim jeans an' maybe a pair of boots. We better take my car 'cause yours looks a lit'l too flashy for Ol' Bobby," Danny adds.

"Whatever you say, my man, whatever you say. I like doin' laundry wit' you. If you want me to get country then let's go get country," Turtle affirms.

A couple hours later, Danny's Ford Escort is flanked by acres of neglected crop fields now filled with high weeds and wild dandelions as it turns off of the two-lane blacktop that snakes and cuts through Spotsylvania County. Looking out the passenger side window and now attired in blue denim jeans and brown leather boots, Turtle nods pleasingly at the vast open fields that's soon to be his. Danny's Escort is slowly traveling down a long dirt road leading towards Mister Lewis' farm. A leaning FOR SALE sign is posted in the ground near the driveway entrance where an old weathered gate barely stands. A short distance away, Mister Lewis sits quietly on the porch of his sun-beaten farmhouse.

Danny brings the car to a stop near the FOR SALE sign. Mister Lewis stands and steps off the porch, meeting Danny and Turtle halfway in the dirt-patch yard.

"Hi ya' doin' there, Bobby! Got some real good news. Finally gotta buyer for ya' farm," Danny greets.

"No shittin'?" Mister Lewis asks while eying Turtle with a curious face.

"No shittin'. This here's Mister Turtle, and he's willing to pay cash money," Danny nods to Mister Lewis.

The old farmer rubs his chin and chews his thoughts for a moment then turns directly to Turtle.

"Mister Turtle, you live 'round here or you ride a bicycle?" Mister Lewis asks.

Turtle is puzzled by the old farmer's question. Danny glances at Turtle's twisted expression and saves him.

"Mister Turtle here is a venture capitalist," Danny awkwardly injects.

"Venture capitalist, huh? Shit, I don't care what ya' do for a livin' but I do care 'bout the farm here. Tell me, Mister Turtle, whatcha plan to do wit' the farm if I sell it to ya'?" Mister Lewis asks.

Turtle inconspicuously glances at Danny for help but Danny only shoots a look that says 'give it your best shot.'

The silence is getting noticeably awkward then abruptly, Turtle blurts, "I'm gonna capitalize on my venture."

After a second or two of dead silence, simultaneously, the old farmer and Danny look at one another and burst into contagious laughter! Unable to restrain himself, Turtle join in with a hearty chuckle.

After sharing the friendly laugh, Mister Lewis reasons, "Ya' know, Danny, I knew yo' daddy and he was a good man and I think you ain't no different than him. So if y'all wanna draw up 'em papers we gotta deal."

Happily, Danny and Turtle offer handshakes to the old farmer as he looks out at his weed-covered fields. With a touch of sadness in his eyes, Mister Lewis solemnly utters, "Yup, I used to grow corn, beans, wheat, but now, as ya' can see, the only thing out there is 'em dandelions. And I let Ma'Raine's grandson go out there and take whatever they need.

Hell, 'em weeds don't mean nothin' to me. But they mean the world to Ma'Raine though."

Minutes later, Danny and Turtle are walking back towards the car. Turtle steps up to the leaning FOR SALE sign and yanks it out of the ground with a game-winning nod.

Chapter Eight

Blue Nova

It's Saturday morning at the Woods' home. The Sheriff, his daughter LaBrea and son Lamar are enjoying their breakfast at the kitchen table. Lamar and LaBrea are dressed to leave the house soon but their father is still attired in his night clothes with a robe draped over his shoulders. Lamar's specially-designed forearm crutches are leaning next to the empty chair beside him. Sheriff Woods yarns as he butters his toast. Lamar looks excited about his plans for the day as he scoops up his last mouthful of scrambled eggs. Simultaneously, LaBrea devours her pop tart and checks her messages on her cellphone. The corner of the pop tart protrudes out of her mouth as her fingers speedily dance over the tiny keypad.

"LaBrea, do you have to mess with your phone while you're eating?" Sheriff Woods sighs.

Mimicking her father's baritone voice, LaBrea utters the familiar words that often follow, "You know that ain't very lady-like."

Amused by his sister's playfulness, Lamar smiles then changes the subject, "I cc..can't ww..wait 'til mm..my loan gg..get approved ss..so I can gg..get my bus."

"Lamar, I don't wanna see you get hurt if that loan don't go through so try to be reasonable and rational about what you wanna do now, alright?" the Sheriff advises.

As if he didn't heard a word his father just said, Lamar nonchalantly responds, "Yup, I ss..should be..gg..gettin' da' money nn..next ww..week."

The Sheriff sighs while reaching for another slice of toast.

"Daddy, I'm gonna be gone all day today. I'm riding my bike over to Ma'Raine's. Me an' Jesse gonna be pickin' dandelions for her," LaBrea injects.

"La..LaBrea, cc..can you see if Jesse cc..can tt..take me to da' hob..hobby ss..shop ww..when he gg..go get da' bb..bottles in tt..town? That'll ss..save me ss..some money from using the tt..taxi bb..both ways," Lamar asks.

"I'll call him right now," LaBrea quickly responds as her fingertips rapidly tap over the small keypad, "Good mornin', loverboy –"

Teasingly, Sheriff Woods spurts out, "Loverboy?"

"Dad!" LaBrea shoots a look then continues on the phone, "Jesse, sorry. My brother wants to know if you can pick him up and take him to the hobby shop if you're going to be picking up the wine bottles in town."

"Lamar, he said to be ready in about an hour," LaBrea nods.

Lamar is all smiles, "Man, tth..that blue Nova is ss..sooo cc..coool."

LaBrea stands then walks over to her father. Lovingly, LaBrea wraps her arms around her dad then rewards him with a tender kiss on his cheek.

"Daddy, you're puttin' on the pounds. Maybe you can use yo' day off to pull yo' bike out the garage an' go for a long ride like me," LaBrea suggests.

Somewhat playfully, the Sheriff slowly turns his head to face his loving daughter then gives her a scornful eye.

"Okay, that's my cue to leave," LaBrea quips.

"Bye!" Lamar utters while reaching for his crutches.

Enjoying his day off, Sheriff Woods methodically places three slices of bacon and a scoop of scrambled eggs atop a piece of toast with a satisfying grin.

❦

Meanwhile, at the Raine's home, Patty sits quietly at the kitchen table sipping her morning coffee. Jesse is gathering up a few items for his day-long job of picking dandelions for his grandmother. The tension in the air is thick. Patty doesn't look at her son as he goes in and out of the kitchen placing various items in plastic grocery bags atop the table. Jesse never makes eye contact with his mother as he places two hand towels and a bottle of water in a bag.

Gazing at the floating clouds in her coffee cup, Patty nervously taps her fingers on the table. Abruptly, she explodes, "What the fuck I'm supposed to do Jesse when you and LaBrea move away? It's not me an' you no more Jesse! It's you an' LaBrea now. So you tell me, Jesse! What the fuck I'm supposed to do, huh?"

Patty hammers the table with her fist! Her coffee cup tumbles over! A river of coffee floods the table! Jesse calmly gathers up the plastic bags at the other end of the table, never turning his head or glances at his hysterical, guilt-ridden mother. With his car keys dangling from his fingertip, Jesse leaves.

A short time later, Jesse's '77 blue Chevy Nova pulls into the Woods' driveway behind the Sheriff's cruiser. Lamar is waiting near the flowerbed and is anxious to hop into that souped-up Nova. Jesse keeps the car running as Lamar opens the passenger door and works his crutches into the back seat then carefully maneuvers himself into the passenger seat. Jesse backs out of the driveway then heads down the backcountry, single-lane blacktop. Lamar runs his hand along the unique instrument panel then smiles admiringly.

"So whatcha been up to, Lamar?" Jesse asks.

"Just ww..waitin' on a loan ff..for my shuttle bb.. bus bb..business," Lamar answers.

"That's right, LaBrea did tell me you wanted to do some'em to help the poor folks out here who didn't have a ride into town. Sounds like you'd be a good politician. Lamar, won'tcha run for one of 'em county seats or some'em, " Jesse suggests.

"Naw, I ain't nn..no Ba..Barack Obama. I jj..just ww..wanna dr..drive my bb..bus," Lamar replies.

Amused, Jesse cracks a smile then adds, "Tell ya' what, Lamar, if you need another driver for your shuttle business you can count on me."

"Ooo...o'kay," Lamar nods.

Jesse's blue Nova makes its way across the bridge leading towards the outskirts of Fredericksburg City. Underneath, the slow-moving Rappahannock River crawls with the snail-pace of these Southern backwoods. Crossing the bridge and passing the huge Serv City Truckstop, Jesse and Lamar continues to downtown Fredericksburg.

Cruising along Caroline Street, the glistening Nova pulls up curbside in front of SMITH'S BOTTLES AND GLASSWARE. A sign in the window professes...

TELL US WHAT YOU NEED
WE MAKE CANDLE HOLDERS,
BOTTLES, CUSTOMIZED ASH
TRAYS, AND JUST ABOUT
ANYTHING!
COME IN AND ASK BUNNY

As Jesse gets out of the car Lamar leans over and wraps his fingers around the steering wheel in a moment of wishful bliss. Jesse enters the shop. Gray-haired Bunny Smith is dusting off animal figurines on a shelf near the cash register. There's a vast assortment of colorful flower vases, jars, candle holders, and other glass décor items of all shapes and sizes on the shelves around the cozy store.

"Mornin', Jesse. There's two boxes over in the corner for you," Bunny greets.

"Hey Bunny," Jesse replies as he proceeds straight to the corner. Repeating this process a couple times a month, Jesse makes it look easy as he places a full box of empty wine bottles atop another then casually lifts the boxes off of the floor.

"Tell Ma'Raine I said hello now," Bunny adds while holding the door open.

"Okay, Bunny. See ya' in two weeks," Jesse replies.

As Jesse steps outside, a red Chevy Impala passes by with two teenage girls upfront. The girl on the passenger side sticks her head out the window and shouts, "Hey Jesse, can I sing backup for you?!"

Jesse grins in response to the fanfare then carefully places the two boxes into the trunk next to the plastic bags he'd taken from his house earlier. He shuts the trunk then hurriedly gets back behind the wheel.

Jesse merges back into the light traffic along Caroline Street.

"Lamar, you're up next," Jesse says.

"Oo..okay," Lamar nods.

Cruising slowly past the numerous specialty shops and boutiques, Jesse brings the sparkling Nova to a snail's pace then makes a U-turn and parks in front of HARRISON'S HOBBY SHOP.

Lamar retrieves his crutches out of the back seat then methodically maneuvers himself out of the car, cautiously gathering his balance.

"Th..thanks..ll..lovv..loverboy," Lamar teases.

"Man, I don't see how yo' sister put up wit' you and yo' dad," Jesse quips then asks, "You gonna be okay gettin' back?"

"Yup. Cab. Sss..see ya', Jesse," Lamar nods.

"Alright an' don't buy the whole store," Jesse jokes then drives away.

Lamar carefully works his way towards the hobby shop door and enters. Plastic airplane mobiles dangle from the ceiling as two young boys excitedly chase a remote-controlled monster truck between the aisles. Lamar steps toward a lengthy counter topped with several display products. Shelves are stocked with vintage toys, train sets, a wide variety of model kits, numerous remote-control vehicles, and all sorts of craft accessories, supplies and miscellaneous items; wood sticks, glue, clay, play dough and various types of fireworks.

Mister Harrison is at the counter making minor adjustments on an advanced F-16 fighter jet model. Nearby, a colossal aircraft carrier ship is proudly displayed atop the counter. Lamar stops and begins to touch several die cast YELLOW SCHOOL BUSES neatly lined up on a middle shelf. Lamar's face illuminates with delight as he plays with the tiny door, softly pushing it in and out with his finger.

Mister Harrison glances over at Lamar getting a kick out of the miniature school buses. Mister Harrison loves to see his regulars happy. His face brightens just the same as Lamar's.

Stepping away from the counter, Mister Harrison turns toward a parcel box sitting on the floor.

"Lamar, com'on over here. I believe your order finally came in," Mister Harrison says.

Lamar maneuvers himself closer as Mister Harrison uses a box cutter to open the box.

Unraveling brown cushion papers, Mister Harrison then retrieves an immaculate blue 1977 Chevy Nova replica!

"Wwwow! Juussst like Jesse's!" Lamar blossoms!

"Ain't that some'em. She's a real beauty," Mister Harrison adds.

Lamar takes a closer look at the model. His face glows as he admires the perfect detail.

"Wwwow!" Lamar nods again.

"Lamar, how's your physical therapy comin' along?" Mister Harrison asks.

"Goo..good. They ss..say mm..muscle need nn.. nerve ee..electric cc..charge. Sss..stim..stimulation they cc..call it," Lamar replies.

"Sounds good, Lamar. That's a good place that VA in Richmond. Uncle Sam's doin' right by y'all. You boys done served, now it's Uncle Sam's turn to serve y'all," Mister Harrison says with a bit of concern in his voice.

Chapter Nine

Knock N Walk

LaBrea is peddling her bike along a lonesome country road. She passes a patch of woods then a stretch of open farm fields. A short distance ahead, the narrow road comes to an end and LaBrea turns right on the connecting two-lane blacktop.

Along the blacktop, LaBrea passes modest country homes dotted with intermittent fields and brief woods. A woman is retrieving her mail from the roadside mailbox and waves hello to LaBrea as she peddles by. Passing another nearby home, a man in his front yard is bending over trying to yank a stubborn dandelion plant out of the ground with his hand. The man's face quickly fills with frustration as the upper-half of the stem snaps off, leaving most of the plant and its root still in the ground. Standing on the porch, the man's wife shakes her head in disbelief while wearing an expression that says 'you stupid idiot.'

LaBrea is all smiles as she enjoys her tranquil bike ride. A little ways up the road, a postal Jeep is parked near a roadside mailbox where newcomer Turtle is angrily pointing his finger in the mailman's face!

Continuing up the road, LaBrea's face becomes puzzled as she hears Turtle's angry, boisterous voice several yards away.

"I ain't gotta putta goddamn name on my mailbox if I don't wanna! It already got the fuckin' rural route number on it an' the damn fuckin' box number on it so why the hell ya' need a goddamn name on it?!" Turtle yells!

Submissively, the mild mannered mailman quietly backs away from the barking Turtle then gets into his Jeep and drives away. Appearing from the side yard, RoRo is wheeling out a barbecue grill towards the middle of the front yard. Nervously, LaBrea peddles her bike past Turtle's house. Turtle's eyes are fixated on LaBrea's shapely butt as she rides by. RoRo quietly watches LaBrea from a distance. He, too, looks at LaBrea with leering eyes. Turtle is only a few feet away from LaBrea. He can't restrain himself and utters, "Damn girl, you gotta beautiful ass! Hey, won'tcha come back later on and have some barbecue ribs with us."

Peddling away, LaBrea doesn't respond.

Turtle turns to his young sidekick and boasts, "Damn RoRo, did you see that fat country ass on that bitch?! Damn!"

"Remember that white dude at school I was tellin' you about? That's his girlfriend," RoRo adds.

Turtle's taken aback.

"Wait a minute now. That fine ass sister gotta white dude hittin' that shit?" Turtle asks.

RoRo nods 'yes' as disbelief spreads across Turtle's face.

"I know," RoRo nods agreeably.

Speeding up, LaBrea is now safely out of Turtle's reach as she continues her morning ride to Ma'Raine's. Minutes later, Jesse's Nova slowly creeps up alongside LaBrea's fast-moving bike. Jesse pokes his head out the window and teasingly flirts with his gorgeous looking girlfriend, "Hey that bike riding really is a good way to exercise. I tell ya' what, when ya' lose a few more pounds give me a call alright?"

Flashing that big cowboy smile of his, Jesse floors the gas! He's long gone before LaBrea has a chance to fire off one of her sarcastic comebacks.

෨෨

Jesse's Nova is parked in his grandmother's driveway with its trunk open. Jesse is carrying the two boxes of bottles across the unkempt yard then up the porch steps where the unlatched screen door swings freely.

Jesse gently places the two boxes of bottles atop the kitchen table. There are two empty straw baskets atop the other end of the table. Jesse walks into a den area adjacent to the kitchen. Seemingly pushed for time, Jesse hurriedly walks over to the corner where a computer and a connected printer are situated. Apparently very familiar with his grandmother's makeshift office, Jesse blindly turns on the computer and begins to feed the printer with sheets of blank, self-adhesive labels. He quickly types the words to be printed on the labels. The computer screen instantly displays…

MA'RAINE'S DANDELION WINE

Jesse scans the printed sheets of labels stacking up on the printer's catch tray. Satisfied with the labels, he shuts off the computer then hastily leaves the den. On his way out, Jesse takes the two straw baskets off of the kitchen then loudly alarms, "Grandma, ya' need to start lockin' ya' doors! See ya' later!"

Pressed for time, Jesse doesn't wait for a response. He leaves as his grandmother yells from behind the closed door of her bedroom, "Jesse, make sure you don't pick 'em wrong kinda' dandelions t'day. You gotta pay attention to whatcha doin' out there now, okay?"

Jesse is already out the house and off the porch. He didn't catch a word of his grandmother's message.

LaBrea's bike is propped against the left side of the porch. She's been patiently waiting for Jesse in the passenger seat of his Nova. Jesse places the two straw baskets into the trunk then quickly gets back behind the wheel. The sparkling blue Chevy backs out of the driveway then heads down the county's two-lane.

❧❦

The noon-day sun is heating up the field Jesse had chosen to work today. The hillside is ornamented with a wide variety of feather grasses and colorful wild flowers. Jesse's Nova is parked off the two-lane's shoulder at the edge of the bountiful field. With their straw baskets in tow, LaBrea and Jesse are slowly stepping through a dense patch of blossomed yellow-head dandelions and plucking the flower heads from the stems then placing them into their baskets. Jesse is not himself. He's blindly plucking off the flower heads, not at all concentrating on the certain type of dandelion in which he should not be picking.

LaBrea and Jesse both have a damp hand towel dangling from their back pants pocket to wipe off the milky sap that oozes out of the dandelion stem when it's broken. Jesse is uncannily quiet. Concerned, LaBrea stops. She wipes the sap from her fingers then glances at Jesse. Slugging along without any spirit whatsoever and unaware of LaBrea's gaze, Jesse seems to be a thousand miles away.

"Some'em wrong, Jesse?" LaBrea asks.

Jesse turns and looks at LaBrea but doesn't say anything. He continues to pluck off another flower head as LaBrea gives him a look and playfully demands, "Jesse Raine, if you don't stop and come talk to me I'm gonna –"

Cutting her off, Jesse solemnly asks, "Wanna take a break?"

Sensing that something heavy is weighing Jesse down, LaBrea tries to divert his thoughts as she steps closer and gently pulls him down to the ground. The partially filled baskets are placed aside as LaBrea intimately nestles herself between Jesse's legs and softly rests her head upon his chest. Jesse straps his muscled arms around LaBrea as she naturally begins to interlock her fingers with his. Reading each other's subtle gestures without speaking a single word and feeling so comfortable together they know that this is something that's meant to be.

After a few minutes of tranquil heaven, Jesse abruptly asks, "LaBrea, would ya' ever sell yourself?"

Always the kidder, LaBrea takes this moment to have a little fun, "I knew you were a pimp from day one. So tell me Mister Pimp Daddy Jesse Raines, how many girls you got workin' for you, huh?"

Jesse's not in the mood for LaBrea's playfulness right now. She turns around and looks at the seriousness in his face. She inches upward and plants a tender kiss on his chin.

"Jesse, what is it?" LaBrea softly asks.

Jesse sighs, "When I was in sixth grade this older kid named Lonnie used to tease me all the time 'bout my mom being everybody's girl, an' back then I didn't even know what he meant by it. Last night I caught my mom at Serv City doin' some'em beside waitin' on tables."

"Some'em like what?" LaBrea asks.

Jesse gives her a knowing look.

Shocked, LaBrea solemnly utters, "Oh, I'm so sorry, Jesse."

LaBrea sees that this revelation has really gotten a tight grip on Jesse so she tries to ease his pain by opening the jar to one of her deepest wounds, "Jesse, we've been together for about a year now and you've been sweet not to ask me about my mother an —"

"Thought it was none of my business," Jesse politely injects in his Southern gentleman's tone.

Once again, LaBrea inches upward and rewards Jesse with another kiss on his chin then continues, "And I never brought my mother up 'cause it still hurts. Daddy was just one of the regular patrol deputies back then and one day he was on patrol near our house so he thought he would just stop by and fix himself some'em for lunch but when he drove up he was surprised to see my mother's car still parked in the driveway 'cause he thought she'd be at work at the hospital. So he goes in the house an' heard noises comin' from their bedroom. He did a knock n' walk an—"

Fighting back tears, LaBrea can't continue. The image is too painful. Jesse can't stand to see LaBrea suffering in any type of manner. He's struggling to find a way to say something or do something to lighten the moment, even if it means that he must absorb and suffer through his own heartache if he unleashes the story that he'd kept bottled up for years.

"Aw, you know who got the best knock n' walk story in Spotsylvania County? I do. Ya' see, befo' my grandma kicked my mama out years ago we all lived there an' Grandma used to have this cat man – that's 'em guys who catch the catfish outta the Rappahannock – visit her every time he gotta day off an'I guess one day Grandma took too long comin' back from somewhere an' did a knock n' walk an' found her naked cat man on top of her sixteen year old daughter," Jesse sighs.

"So your father's the cat man?" LaBrea asks.

"Yup," Jesse nods.

"You ever met him?" LaBrea asks.

Jesse shakes his head 'no' then adds, "I kinda just work it all out through my songs."

The moment is getting a little too heavy for LaBrea.

"I'm gettin' hungry. You got anything in the car?" LaBrea asks while beginning to stand.

"Com'on, we can get burgers at Spotsy's Grill down the road," Jesse suggests while reaching for the two partially-filled baskets of dandelion flower heads.

Chapter Ten

White this Morning

Meanwhile, across the river in the City of Fredericksburg, loan manager Jennifer Day is having coffee and lunch with her older sister Allison at The Coffee Café on Main Street. They are seated at a small table near the window. Allison is a spirited soccer mom. She is carrying on about her kids' performance in their latest game. Jennifer's mind is elsewhere as she gazes out the window and sips her coffee while Allison goes on and on about her kids, "And Sherry was all over that ball when Kyle just came out of nowhere and —"

"Allison, do you know where I can buy a bus?" Jennifer abruptly asks.

Puzzled, Allison shoots her sister a look then utters, "What?"

"Not a new bus. Maybe like an old school bus or a used church bus," Jennifer explains.

"A bus? Why?" Allison questions.

Jennifer ignores the questions and insists, "You know a lot of people in town, Allison. I know you must know some –"

"You're serious, aren't you?" Allison injects.

Jennifer nods 'yes.'

"There's this one big place, Johnny's, I think. It's kind of a junkyard but they sell some of the stuff they repair. The school district gets rid of their old buses there," Allison says.

Excitedly, Jennifer springs up!

"Great! Where is it?!" Jennifer asks.

"Out on Plank Road," Allison answers as Jennifer gives her a quick 'thank you' and goodbye hug then hurries out the door!

Baffled, Allison shakes her head.

☙❧

Back across the bridge at SPOTSY'S GRILL, Jesse's blue Nova pulls into the nearly-full parking lot the popular roadside diner. Holding hands, LaBrea and Jesse walks in. Nearly every table and booth is occupied with customers. A table of two elderly white couples is near the entrance. Rudely, the four seniors begin to stare at the young lovebirds holding hands. Looks of distaste begin to surface on their crusty, wrinkled faces.

LaBrea and Jesse have encountered this situation periodically over the past year. Jesse coolly winks at LaBrea to let her know that he'll handle these old, narrow-minded Southerners. Jesse steps up to the edge of the seniors' table. Slowly he lowers his head, one at a time looks each of them straight in the eye and then softly whispers, "Well shit in my pants y'all, I can't figure it out. She was white this morning."

Jesse smoothly steps away, leaving the four seniors with shocked, bitter faces.

A waitress approaches LaBrea and Jesse then leads them to a vacant booth along the right side wall. As she would normally do for a dining couple, the waitress places their placemats directly across from the other atop the table. LaBrea slides in, and to the waitress' surprise, Jesse slides in the booth right beside LaBrea. The waitress quickly corrects the placement of the placemats then smiles admirably at the young lovebirds sitting side by side.

LaBrea shares a warm smile with the friendly waitress then jokes, "Trust me, he don't sit beside me like this because he loves me or anything like that. He just sits like this 'cause it's easier for him to take my food."

"Would y'all like a menu?" the waitress asks.

Jesse glances at LaBrea as she shakes her head 'no.'

"We'll both take a cheeseburger an' fries with cream soda," Jesse says.

"You got it," the perky waitress quickly utters then steps away.

Quite a few tables away near the entrance, two of the white seniors are nosily looking at Jesse and LaBrea then shaking their heads in repulsion. LaBrea notices the old Southerners gazing at them. Their rude stares trigger LaBrea to think about things between her and Jesse. She looks at Jesse as if she wants to say something but doesn't, then awkwardly she bluntly asks, "Jesse, if you was ever at the Country Music Awards on national TV and had to go up on stage to accept an award, would you publicly acknowledge me to all ' your fans?"

"Wow, where did that come from?" Jesse asks.

"Com'on, I really need to know your answer," LaBrea insists.

"First of all, my fans would've already gotten to know who you are 'cause they would've seen you already on the cover of my first CD. And about gettin' up on stage at the Awards show, not only would I have ya' come on up wit' me, but I'll have our daughter Jesla join us up there too," Jesse proudly nods.

Wearing an amused grin, LaBrea asks, "Our daughter? Jesla?"

"Yup. Jesla. She'll have a piece of my name and a piece of your name. Jesla," Jesse nods again.

"What if we have a boy?" LaBrea teasingly asks.

"They tell me ' the man determines the sex of the baby an' I've decided that we're gonna have a daughter first," Jesse quips.

The playful lovebirds enjoy a light chuckle then LaBrea plants a soft kiss on Jesse's lips.

"You're crazy, you know that? Just plain country crazy," LaBrea teases.

"Hey, I been workin' on a new song," Jesse says.

"What's it called?"

"Changin' Face."

Nodding approvingly, LaBrea utters, "Hm. I like the title. What's –"

Suddenly, the waitress returns with their food: cheeseburgers, fries and cream soda.

"There's ketchup and mustard on the table. Can I get y'all anything else?" the waitress pleasantly asks.

Simultaneously, the lovebirds nod 'no.' While sprinkling salt on his fries, Jesse glances at LaBrea through the corner of his eyes. LaBrea's unaware of Jesse's glance as she lifts the bun and squirts more ketchup on her cheeseburger.

"Still thinkin' about goin' to the University of Maryland after graduation?" Jesse abruptly asks.

"Jesse, I really like their program. And it's not even that far. It's like two hours away," LaBrea sighs.

"If I win this talent show over at Serv City, I'm takin' the prize money to make a real good demo an' shop it around Nashville," Jesse says.

"I thought you had enough money saved up for the demo from what Ma'Raine gives you," LaBrea questions.

"Nah, I got my new guitar wit' that money," Jesse explains.

"Hm. Sounds like you need a financial planner," LaBrea quips.

"Yo' brother is my backup plan," Jesse injects.

Puzzled, LaBrea gives Jesse a look.

"When he gets his shuttle bus operation runnin' then I can drive part time for 'em," Jesse adds.

Amused, LaBrea spreads a long smile then suggests, "Com'on, eat ya' food. We still gotta lot more dandelions to pick."

Chapter Eleven

65 Mustang

On the outer edge of Fredericksburg, the choppy, graveled Plank Road leads into the massive yard of JOHNNY'S SALVAGE AND SALES. The back lots and sprawling hillside are carpeted with countless rows of wrecked and partially dismantled vehicles of all types: trucks, cars, SUV's, vans and buses.

Near the entrance, on the right side of the office and an adjacent garage, there's a line of vehicles with a 'For Sale' sign posted in each windshield. Two aging school buses, three late-model sedans and a beat-up rusty station wagon are available for purchase. The legs of Raul, the mechanic, are protruding from underneath a jacked up car in the garage. He's tightening a bolt on the rear axle. Jennifer Day's lime-green Dodge Neon pulls up in front of the garage. She steps out and immediately walks over to one of the two buses displaying its 'For Sale' sign. An endless smile of relief glows on Jennifer's face as she hastily walks around the bus. A wide band of black paint now covers the once-visible letters on the bus rust-spotted side panels. Raul scoots out from under the car in the garage. He notices Jennifer looking at the old school bus and begins to wipe his greasy hands with the dangling rag tucked in the side pocket of his soiled overalls. Raul walks out of the garage towards Jennifer. The cheerful-hearted mechanic asks Jennifer in his best broken English, "You like?"

"How much for this bus?" Jennifer responds.

"Two thousand ' that one," then pointing to the other bus, "three thousand ' that one," Raul answers.

"Both run good. Me fix 'em good," Raul adds.

"Hm. Are you Johnny?" Jennifer asks.

"Me Raul. Johnny ' me boss. Johnny go Atlantic City. He say he play blackjack an' come back ' millionaire. Johnny say me in charge 'til he come back millionaire," Raul explains.

"So if my friend came here and gives you two thousand dollars, he can get this bus?" Jennifer questions.

"Yo' friend ' my friend. Bring two thousand – friend take bus. You happy, me happy, friend happy, Johnny happy," Raul quips.

Another joyful grin quickly spreads across Jennifer's face.

"My friend will be seeing you like real soon!" Jennifer excitedly says while rushing back to her car.

"Me be here," Raul nods and waves goodbye as Jennifer backs up and speedily drives away.

Jennifer spends the next two hours going place to place desperately trying to raise two thousand dollars in cash. At home in her bedroom, Jennifer hastily dumps out her jewelry box. Hurriedly, she picks through the mixed pile of sparkling necklaces, earrings and bracelets then tosses a few selected pieces into her purse.

At an ATM kiosk on Main Street, Jennifer retrieves a small stack of twenty dollar bills from the catch tray.

A short time later, at a pawn shop along Caroline Street, Jennifer's jewelry is spread out atop the glass counter as the owner looks on. The owner's professional eyes quickly scan the spread. He shrugs his shoulders and quotes her an offer. Reluctantly, Jennifer nods 'yes' as the owner happily digs out a fat wad of bills from his pants pocket then begins to peel off several fifty and hundred dollar bills for Jennifer.

At the bustling Food Lion supermarket, Jennifer is at the checkout stand with an anxious herd of shoppers in line behind her with overflowing baskets. Nonchalantly, Jennifer places a small pack of gum on the conveyor belt then positions her debit card to swipe. The cashier scans the pack of gum then asks, "Any cash back?"

"What's the max I can get back?" Jennifer asks.

Concealing a dirty look behind an awkward, forced smile, the cashier answers, "One hundred."

Jennifer quickly nods, "A hundred."

Slyly, the cashier gives Jennifer a condescending look then gestures her to swipe her debit card. Jennifer swipes her card then enters her PIN number. The cashier hands Jennifer her receipt, small pack of gum and five twenty dollar bills while donning a disdainful smirk.

❦

Across the bridge, the County Sheriff is still enjoying his day off. Sheriff Woods is comfortably attired in his blue jeans and T-shirt spraying a liquid pesticide on persistent dandelions sprouting up all over his otherwise plush, green front lawn. Jennifer's lime-green Dodge Neon pulls up in the driveway and crawls to a stop behind the Sheriff's cruiser. Jennifer steps out with her stuffed purse tucked under her arm.

Sheriff Woods gazes at the loud colored Neon with an admiring grin.

"I sho' do like that color! I once had a Plymouth Duster that same color some years ago. How ya' doin'?" the Sheriff greets.

"Fine, thank you. I'm Jenny. Is there a Lamar Woods here? " Jennifer asks.

Sheriff Woods lowers the gallon-container of pesticide and mini-sprayer to the ground. Stepping closer to Jennifer, the Sheriff cordially adds, "Hi, Jenny. People call me Woody. Lamar's my son. He went into town. He'll be –"

The Sheriff is momentarily distracted by a taxi turning off of the blacktop.

"That's him now," the Sheriff continues.

The taxi briefly parks behind Jennifer's Dodge Neon. The bottom end of Lamar's aluminum crutches begin to protrude from the taxi's rear door. A plastic bag dangles from Lamar's fingertips as he struggles to stand and gathers his balance on the crutches.

Now standing, Lamar kicks the taxi door shut with one of his crutches.

The taxi drives away. Lamar notices Jennifer standing beside his dad near the driveway. Utterly surprised, Lamar excitedly shouts, "Jen..Jennifer! Ooops, I mm..mean Jen..Jenny!"

Jennifer walks over and gives Lamar a warm hug as her bulging purse dangles from her right hand. Suspiciously, Jennifer speaks softly into Lamar's ear, "I came here to tell you some good news about your loan, Lamar. Can we talk privately somewhere?"

"Yup..th..then ya' cc..can ss..see mm..my ss.. sixty-five Mm..Mus..Mustang," Lamar answers Jennifer in his usual tone and catches his father's attention as well.

Assuming that Lamar meant that they could sit privately in his car, perhaps parked in the garage or possibly parked in the backyard, Jennifer turns her head every which way looking for Lamar's '65 Mustang.

"Is it in the garage? In the backyard?" she asks.

Eavesdropping on his son's conversation, the Sheriff cracks a smile as he anticipates Lamar's response.

"Nope. In mm..my room," Lamar answers.

"Your room?" Jennifer sighs.

Lamar carefully steps toward the front door then nods to Jennifer, "Cc..com'on."

Wearing a curious expression, Jennifer follows Lamar into the house. Picking up the container of pesticide and its attached spray gun, the Sheriff nods amusingly at the realization that his son have gotten the attention of a fine young woman.

Lamar leads Jennifer into his colorful sanctuary, his bedroom. Jennifer is awestruck as she gaze around the vibrant room. A tall bookshelf stretches the full length of the left wall. Every inch of the multi-layer bookshelf is occupied with a vintage model car: '69 Roadrunner, '74 Duster, '62 Impala, '68 Pontiac GTO, '69 Camaro, '67 Volks Wagon, '66 Corvett, ect. Over two hundred different models make up Lamar's elaborate collection. Proudly displayed on the middle shelf and enclosed in a glass case is Lamar's most-prized possession, a classic red 1965 Ford Mustang. Lamar gestures Jennifer to take a closer look at the encased Mustang but something else has captured her attention.

On the rightside wall are several 8X10 framed photos of Lamar attired in his desert camouflage uniform standing next to his comrades of their Army demolition unit. The backdrop in each photo is of a different, recently-bombarded structure in Iraq. Jennifer is taking a serious interest in the framed pictures. She can't seem to take her eyes off of them. The photos of Lamar and fellow uniformed soldiers have triggered something deep inside of her.

Lamar tosses the plastic bag that he was carrying atop his bed. He leans his crutches against the nearby nightstand then lowers himself on the bed. He retrieves the contents from the bag, revealing his latest additions to his majestic collection, a replica of Jesse's '77 Chevy Nova and a DIE CAST YELLOW SCHOOL BUS.

"Ss..so, I gg..got da' loan?" Lamar asks while startling Jennifer.

"Oh, I'm sorry," Jennifer utters as she turns around.

She retrieves a stuffed envelope out of her purse then hands it to Lamar.

"Congratulations, Lamar! Your loan application has been officially approved and I wanted to, personally, bring you the money myself. There's two thousand dollars in there along with a note detailing the name and address of the place where you can get that first bus to start your very own commuter shuttle business!" Jennifer cheerfully adds.

"Th..thank you. Bbb..but ww..what about da' pp..payment pp..plan?" Lamar asks.

Caught off-guard, Jennifer has to think of something quick. Awkwardly, she blurts, "There's none. No payment plan at all. You see, Lamar, you had qualified for this special loan where you don't have to pay anything back. I guess it's more like a grant than a loan."

Once again, Jennifer turns around and gaze at the various Army photos on the wall. A bit puzzled, Lamar asks, "Ss..some kinda mm..mil..military thing?"

"Yep. A military thing," Jennifer quickly nods then, with an inviting smile, she adds, "Lamar, would you like to come to my place and have dinner with me later this evening? I can pick you up."

Spreading a triumphant grin, Lamar boasts, "Bbb..boy, tt..today is mm..my lucky dd..day!"

"Great. I'll come by 'round seven or so," Jennifer says while giving Lamar a goodbye hug.

"Th..thanks again ff..for hh..helping mm..me ww..with da' loan, Jen..Jenny," Lamar utters.

"My pleasure. See ya' at seven," Jennifer replies while stepping out.

Chapter Twelve

Bad Petals

Jesse's glistening blue Nova arrives in Ma'Raine's driveway. LaBrea's bike is where she'd left it earlier this morning, leaning against the side of the porch. Jesse and LaBrea removes the two baskets of yellow dandelion flower heads from the trunk then takes them into the house.

Ma'Raine is busy in her kitchen prepping the necessary ingredients for the next batch of her popular homemade dandelion wine. Her method is handled in very specific stages, and her kitchen is meticulously organized. A large pot of water is being heated atop the stove. Fresh lemons and oranges sit in a basket on the kitchen table. A bag of sugar and a container of yeast are positioned near two large bowls. A space on the table is made for the incoming baskets from Jesse.

Doing this for a number of years now, Ma'Raine's homemade process has become a simple science and her kitchen is her laboratory. The materials for the final bottling stage are set aside. In the far corner are the two boxes of empty bottles that Jesse had dropped off earlier, a bag of corks, sheets of self-adhesive printed labels and two funnels.

Jesse and LaBrea walks in and places the straw baskets of flower heads on the table.

Ma'Raine immediately walks over to inspect the flower heads. She doesn't look happy.

"Hello, Ma'Raine," LaBrea breaks the ice.

Ma'Raine ignores LaBrea and begins to bark at her grandson, "What took you so long, Jesse? How many times I gotta tell ya' the petals can't be sittin' out for long periods of time? They lose their flavor that way, Jesse!"

Ma'Raine's fingers dig deeper into the baskets. She quickly scans a few more dandelion heads, and this time, she shoots Jesse a harden, contemptuous eye.

LaBrea tries again, "Hello, Ma'Ra—"

"You been wit' Jesse all day?" Ma'Raine scornfully asks.

LaBrea nods 'yes.'

Expecting that answer from LaBrea, once again, Ma'Raine goes after Jesse.

"Damn it, Jesse!" Ma'Raine growls!

Respectfully, Jesse never talks back to his grandmother. Submissively, he absorbs her verbal beating as LaBrea stands helplessly nearby.

"Some of these is the wrong kind! Didn't ya' hear me when ya' left here this mornin'? I told ya' not to pick the wrong ones! 'Em false dandelions gotta bad taste! They mess up everything! I can't use 'em! What was y'all doin' out there all day?" Ma'Raine rips!

LaBrea gestures to Jesse that she wants to leave and begins to quietly back out of the kitchen as Ma'Raine continues to tear into Jesse, "You should've spent more time concentrating on what ya' supposed to be doin' instead of tryin' to get between LaBrea's legs! That's what's wrong wit' this country now! Everybody's so damn busy tryin' to get between somebody's legs instead of doin' what they should be doin'! If ya' just do whatcha susposed to be doin' in da' first place then somebody's gonna open their legs up for ya' anyway."

Jesse remains humble. He's been helping his grandmother ever since he was able to walk, and he knows when to open his mouth, and more importantly, when not to.

Knowing the specific steps of Ma'Raine's homemade process, Jesse, without being asked, begins to pluck the yellow petals off of the flower heads then let the loose petals drop into one of the large empty bowls atop the table.

Still pissed, Ma'Raine releases more steam, "Don't put the bad petals in that bowl! And throw 'em bad flowers in da' trash. I know ya' know da' good ones from 'em fake ones! Ya' need to pay more attention to whatcha doin' next time, Jesse."

"Yes, Grandma," Jesse softly nods.

Meanwhile, outside in the front yard, LaBrea is on her bike pedaling past Jesse's Nova then out of the driveway. She turns onto the two-lane blacktop to begin her long ride home.

ᘒᘔ

Parked in his driveway, Turtle's Cadillac Escalade glistens in the afternoon sun. In the front yard, smoke escapes from the barbecue grill. Turtle and his young sidekick RoRo are standing over the smoky grill having a friendly discussion about the proper techniques of outdoor grilling. RoRo is using a long-handle fork to place a t-bone steak in the center of the grill where an orange fiery flame suddenly shoots upward.

"See, that's the problem wit' you young dogs. You can't put the meat on a hot flame 'cause it's gonna burn the outside too fast," Turtle schools RoRo while moving the t-bone steak from the center to the outer edge of the grill with long-handle tongs.

"See, that's how it's done old school! You wanna put things on low an' take it nice an' real sloooow!"

Turtle laughs while thrusting his thighs and slowly gyrating his hips in a sexual motion.

"Man, you ' crazy," RoRo utters with an amused grin.

Away from the bellowing smoke, Angie is stretched out on a comfortable lounge chair enjoying a peaceful afternoon nap.

Pedaling down the two-lane blacktop, LaBrea is slowly approaching Turtle's house. Turtle and RoRo spots LaBrea on her bike.

"Mmm, I like to getta piece of that juicy steak!" Turtle boasts while cupping his crotch.

"You're not the only one," RoRo nods.

Suddenly, Turtle begins to shove RoRo out towards the edge of the blacktop.

"Whatcha doin'?" RoRo asks.

"Fishin'. She knows you RoRo so be the bait," Turtle quickly explains.

RoRo nods agreeably as Turtle walks back to the grill.

RoRo stands alone at the edge of the yard. He puts on a phony, friendly face as LaBrea gets closer. Strategically, RoRo steps out into the road to block LaBrea's path as she comes within a few feet away.

LaBrea stops. In the background, through a mist of bellowing smoke, Turtle is admiring LaBrea's womanly curves.

"Hey, LaBrea. Remember me? I'm in your horticulture class," RoRo greets with an awkward smile.

LaBrea never liked RoRo since the first day he arrived at Spotsylvania High, and it's obvious to her now that his friendly demeanor is fake. Raised with good Southern values, LaBrea forces herself to be cordial.

"Yeah, you're Roland, right?" LaBrea politely responds.

"RoRo, please. So I see you're into that exercise thing, huh?" Roland asks.

"Just a little biking on the weekends or whenever I can," LaBrea answers.

While poking at the various meats on the grill, Turtle glances at RoRo and nods pleasingly at his performance thusfar.

"Look, I know you're probably busy an' gotta go but remember the written test we got comin' up about the differences between the common dandelion and the false dandelion?" RoRo asks.

LaBrea nods 'yes' as RoRo adds, "I get kinda' confused with that stuff. Can you please, pretty please, help me an' kinda' show me the difference again? We gotta lot of dandelions in the back here. Please, LaBrea? Pretty pretty pretty please?"

"Alright, but I can't stay long," LaBrea says.

Overdramatically, RoRo sighs, "Thanks. I really appreciate this."

LaBrea lays her bike down in the grass then walks across the lawn with RoRo.

Slyly, RoRo makes eye contact with Turtle standing near the smoky grill. Turtle responds with another pleasing nod. LaBrea is unaware of the sneakish glances and gestures around her. As RoRo and LaBrea disappear to the backyard, Turtle creatively finds a way to get rid of Angie. He digs out the Escalade's keys and some crumbled bills from his pants pocket then walks up to the lounge chair.

Lightly tapping her shoulder, Turtle utters, "Angie. Angie."

Waking up, Angie asks, "Food ready?"

Somewhat rudely, Turtle drops the keys and wrinkled bills on Angie's lap.

"Baby, we ' gonna need some more steaks," Turtle says.

Angie notices the bicycle lying in the grass.

"Whose bike?" Angie asks.

Short-fusedTurtle is not in the mood for questions from Angie right now. He shoots her a look. With or without words, Turtle has full control over Angie. She knows not to pry. She learned the hard way four years ago after she'd unintentionally lit Turtle's explosive fuse when she skimmed a grand from their sophomoric trick operation at a truck-stop near the DC beltway. Still, to this day, Turtle never lets Angie forget about that money although she has long since paid off that debt many times over.

Reluctantly, Angie struggles up from the comfy lounge chair. With keys and a few wrinkled bills in her hands, she walks across the yard and climbs into the sparkling Escalade. As Angie backs up and drives away, Turtle hurriedly removes the cooked meats off of the grill and tosses them into a nearby pan then hastily covers the sizzling meats with aluminum foil. Not wasting any time, Turtle goes around the house towards the back.

In the backyard, LaBrea is bending over to snap off the stem of a multi-branch dandelion plant.

Educating RoRo, LaBrea explains, "The stem on this one branches out."

RoRo has no interest in LaBrea's lecture, but he has his eyes glued on her shapely butt, unbeknownst to her.

Springing up, LaBrea continues, "It's a solid stem so this is a false dand—"

Startled, LaBrea freezes as she sees Turtle turning the corner. He's looking at her with leering eyes. Apprehension invades LaBrea's cringing face. The dandelion stem slips from her stiffen fingers as she takes a step to leave.

"I gotta go now. See you at school, Roland. Sorry, I mean RoRo," LaBrea nervously utters.

Turtle quickly moves closer to block LaBrea's path and gestures RoRo to do the same. RoRo steps directly behind LaBrea. She's boxed in. Nowhere to turn. Turtle slowly runs his hand along LaBrea's right thigh. LaBrea tries to push Turtle away but he barely budges. Turtle cracks a crooked smile at LaBrea's futile resistance.

"I hear you go for 'em white boys. You one of 'em sisters who think you ' too good for a brother, huh?" Turtle snarls as his hand presses firmly on LaBrea's left thigh.

Turtle inches closer to LaBrea. He's nearly nose-to-nose to her. LaBrea turns her face to avoid his menacing eyes. Inconspicuously, Turtle gives a quick nod to RoRo, signaling him to get ready to make his move. Turtle lowers his hand between LaBrea's thighs and gently massages her crotch. LaBrea spits in Turtle's face! RoRo wraps his arms around her as she tries to wiggle and loosen his grip. LaBrea's no match for Turtle and RoRo.

She's easily manhandled. Turtle wipes the gooey saliva from his face then, with full strength, he hurls a hard backhand across LaBrea's face! She cries in pain then deflates in RoRo's tighten grip. She's nearly unconscious.

"Inside!" Turtle barks at RoRo.

Turtle bends over to grab LaBrea's ankles as RoRo maintains his hold on her upper body. They easily carry her through the back door and into the house.

Half conscious, LaBrea is being carried across the kitchen by RoRo at one end and Turtle at the other. Her vision is somewhat blurred but she's able to make out the coffee cup within arm's reach atop the edge of the kitchen table.

"Man, I'm gonna fuck the hell outta this bitch!" RoRo boasts.

Turtle quickly injects, "After I –"

Suddenly, the soaring coffee cup smashes into Turtle's head! Instantly, Turtle stumbles while grabbing his head in pain, "Aaagh…shit!"

LaBrea's legs drop to the floor! In the excitement, RoRo loses his grip! LaBrea frantically crawls away across the kitchen floor! The coffee cup is incidentally kicked by LaBrea's fast-moving legs and tumbles near Turtle. RoRo quickly leaps atop LaBrea! She's too weak to fight him off of her. Turtle picks up the coffee cup. He grips the cup like a pitcher gripping a baseball then eagle-eyes LaBrea from across the floor.

"Turn her over!" Turtle orders.

LaBrea is exhausted. RoRo turns her over with ease. Turtle walks over and slams the coffee cup on LaBrea's forehead! She moans in agonizing pain as blood splatters everywhere!

"RoRo, drag her ass in yo' room!" Turtle growls.

Obediently, RoRo grabs LaBrea's ankles and drags her across the linoleum as she groans and oozing blood streaks from the gash on her forehead.

RoRo and Turtle tosses LaBrea upon the bed. Like wild savages they rip and tear off her clothes! Turtle unsnaps his pants, lowers his drawers then climbs on top of LaBrea as RoRo watches with hungry eyes.

"Man, get the fuck outta here! Don't worry, you can hit it after I'm done. Won'tcha go clean up the shit in the kitchen an' get rid of the bike in the yard befo' Angie gets back," Turtle suggests.

Reluctantly, RoRo leaves the room. LaBrea is drifting in and out of consciousness. She can barely keep her eyelids from falling shut as Turtle spreads her legs wider across the bed. He strains with all of his might as his brown ass slowly pumps back and forth between her open thighs, "Mmmm! Damn girl, you got some good ass country pussy! Mmmm!"

Outside, in the front yard, RoRo stands up LaBrea's bicycle then hurriedly walks it around to the side of the house towards the back. RoRo is unsure of what to do with the bike. He looks around then focuses on the field of high weeds borderlining the backyard.

RoRo walks the bike through several yards of weeds then gives the bike a strong push! The bike travels several yards upright, abruptly wobbles then crashes to the ground, now hidden in the tall, grassy overgrowth.

Chapter Thirteen

Do What
We Gotta Do

Returning from the store, Angie pulls into the driveway. Turtle is standing near the driveway. He seems overly anxious. A master at manipulating his younger sidekicks, Turtle smoothly puts a guilt trip on Angie with a peculiar look as she steps out of the Escalade dangling the keys and a grocery bag of fresh-cut steaks.

Shooting Turtle a look, Angie argues, "What? I took too long? They had a long line at –"

"I just missed you, baby. How about a lit'l sugar befo' we hit 'em steaks?" Turtle interjects while slyly taking the Escalade's keys from her hand.

Turtle teases and seduces Angie with soft kisses on her neck while smoothly leading her towards the front door of the house. Out of Angie's view, RoRo is peeping around the side of the house. Sneakily, Turtle tosses RoRo the keys as he eases Angie into the house.

The butt of Turtle's .44 Magnum is protruding from RoRo's waistband. Hurriedly, RoRo drags LaBrea across the front lawn. Her tattered, blood-soaked clothes have been loosely put back. Her face is heavily bruised and swollen.

RoRo lifts LaBrea's listless body into the backseat of the Escalade then quickly backs up and drives away.

ʚ|ɞ

A few minutes later, somewhere in Spotsylvania's deep woods, RoRo drives the shiny Escalade through a rugged hunter's path. Thick underbrush, protruding twigs and low-lying branches scrape the sides of the wide-body SUV as it speedily makes its way through the narrow pathway.

RoRo brings the beefy Cadillac to a stop near a small clearing amidst the dense forest of towering oaks, loafty pines and leafydogwoods. RoRo pulls LaBrea out of the backseat then carelessly drops her to the ground where she groans in pain and slightly moves on a bed of wet leaves and fallen twigs. As discussed and instructed by Turtle after they'd both had their way with LaBrea, RoRo now yanks out the .44 Magnum from his waistband then aims it directly at LaBrea's head! Nervously, his hand shivers. He breathes hard then, abruptly, he sighs. He can't do it. Unlike Turtle, deep down, RoRo still has a heart.

RoRo tucks the gun under his waistband then hops back into the Escalade. He backs up, turns around then heads back down the narrow path as, once again, the protruding branches and underbrush scrape the sides of the broad SUV as it slowly fades away. Desperately clinging to life, LaBrea lifts her head and digs her fingers into the damp soil then tries to crawl. She barely moves. She's too weak. Then suddenly, LaBrea's swollen face sinks into the moisten leaves and twigs.

❦

Later in the evening, at her cozy bungalow on Amelia Street, Jennifer Day is in the kitchen preparing after-dinner desserts for her guest.

Seemingly, the living room has been made into some type of shrine. Framed 8X10 pictures ornament the walls. Each photo contains a common theme: a Marine Corps soldier. Similar to the framed pictures gracing the walls of Lamar's bedroom, these photos also have the dry, battle-torn landscape of Iraq as the backdrop. Most of the numerous pictures covering Jennifer's front room shows the young soldier in his desert cammies posing with others in his unit or posing alone with various weaponry: M2 Bradley tank, M19 tripod Browning machine gun, semi-automatic AK-47, M32 grenade launcher, ect...

Patiently sitting on the sofa, Lamar looks around the room at the various photos. His crutches are leaning against the end of a lengthy coffee table. Centered atop the coffee table is a thick photo album labeled 'DONNY.' Jennifer enters the room carrying a tray of brownies and two small glasses of red wine. She places the tray on the coffee table next to the photo album then plants herself snugly beside Lamar.

"How about a little dessert?" Jennifer offers.

"First th..the..pork cc..chops an' nn..now bb.. brownies. I ww..wwanna mm..marry you, Jen.. Jenny," Lamar quips.

Amused, Jennifer grins as Lamar takes a brownie from the tray.

Chewing in absolute delight, Lamar isn't verbally shy about expressing his love for chocolate fudge brownies, "Mmmmmm...mmmmm...mmmmm."

Water begins to film upon Jennifer eyes as she reminisces, "Hm. My Donny would do the same thing. He'd make those same silly sounds too when he ate. My sister keep tellin' me to take all these pictures of Donny down and put this scrapbook up but," Jennifer gently glides her fingers along the top of the photo album, "I just can't do it. I don't know how. I knew Donny since fifth grade. We got married the same day we graduated from high school. He called me his pretty diploma. Hm, James Monroe High.The Yellow Jackets. Donny loved those Friday night football games, especially when the Spotsylvania Knights came to town. I don't think he missed a game 'til he got shipped off to Iraq. I just don't know how to bury him. Just don't know."

The loss of her husband has taken its toll on Jennifer. The lingering memories are overwhelming. She softly rests her head upon Lamar's shoulder.

Lamar hasn't experienced moments like this in a very long time. He stiffens, not truly knowing what to do. Tears begin to trickle from Jennifer's eyes as she takes Lamar's arm and gently places it over her shoulder. Lamar likes the way this feels.

He smiles. Abruptly, Lamar's cellphone rings. He fishes out his phone.

"Hello……..Naw…..O'kay, Jesse," Lamar says with a worrisome face.

"Is everything okay, Lamar?" Jennifer asks as Lamar tucks his phone away.

"My ss..sister's not home yy..yet," Lamar answers.

"Should I take you home now?" Jennifer suggests.

Lamar shakes his head 'no' then adds, "I cc..can hold you ss..some mo' if you ww..want me to."

Jennifer nestles against Lamar's chest as he wraps his arms around her soft, warm body.

"This is nice. Thank you, Lamar," Jennifer softly utters.

Grinning a mile long, Lamar quickly answers, "Wel..welcome."

❦

The Escalade is moving fast along the bridge. Turtle's behind the wheel. There's a noticeable seriousness in Turtle's face, a certain seriousness not often seen. As they cross the bridge heading into Fredericksburg, Angie sits in the passenger seat gazing out the window at the mighty Rappahannock below. Turtle glances in the rear view mirror at RoRo sitting in the back. Looking a little edgy, RoRo slightly turns his head to peer out the window,and purposely avoid eye contact with Turtle.

"Don't sweat it, RoRo. Sometimes we do what we gotta do," Turtle boasts.

RoRo nods his head, leading Turtle to believe that he'd completed 'the job' in the woods earlier today.

"Talkin' in codes?" Angie injects.

Turtle shoots Angie a look then barks, "Who da' fuck ' runnin' this shit?"

Angie rolls her eyes.

Glancing in the rear view mirror at RoRo, Turtle preaches, "You ' my boy, RoRo. You're a true dog, through an' through. You drop for me. I drop for you. Now it's time to upgrade, dog. Every vice president needs his own piece. Right, dog?"

Half-heartedly, RoRo nods 'yes.'

Crossing the bridge to the edge of the city, Turtle continues downtown. A few minutes later, the shiny Escalade parks in front of THE HUNTERS' DEN at 192 William Street. In the window, a flickering neon 'OPEN' sign suddenly goes black. The owner steps outside and begins to lock the door. He's a big, back-wooded man who quietly operates his shop on both sides of the law. Turtle blows the horn! Beep! Beep! Beep! Turtle jumps out of the Escalade and hurries to catch the owner near the door.

"Yo! Can ya' give us ten minutes?" Turtle pleads.

Turtle pulls out a thick wad of hundred dollar bills from his pants pocket then coolly flashes it.

"I'll make it worth yo' while," Turtle nods.

Speaking in a heavy Southern drawl, the shop owner asks, "Whatcha need?"

"Just a lit'l hand piece," Turtle quickly replies.

The brawny shop owner gives Turtle a knowing look. The look Turtle had seen a million times before on the back streets of Washington, DC, a hustler's look.

"Gonna cost ya' extra if ya' don't want no papers," the owner explains.

"No problem," Turtle nods.

As the lofty owner turns around to unlock the door, Turtle gestures RoRo to get out and come join him inside the store. Reluctantly, RoRo steps out of the Escalade, trying his best to conceal an unenthused expression.

The round-bellied owner steps inside the shop. He flips the light switch then codes the keypad on the wall to turn off the alarm. Turtle and RoRo steps inside. Various caliber Winchester hunting rifles and several stuffed deer heads are displayed and mounted on the walls. A locked glass counter running nearly the length of the store encases boxed bullets of different calibers and various brands of handguns: Beretta, Colt, Remington, Ruger, ect...

Shelves of outdoor gear and hunting accessories occupy the opposite side of the shop. The big belly owner points to the variety of handguns on display in the glass case and cordially nods, "Y'all take a peep at these an' let me know whatcha like."

Turtle taps RoRo to look at a certain pistol that he likes.

"Ain't that sweet, dog?" Turtle suggests.

RoRo eyes the gun then puts on an agreeable face.

"How 'bout this bad boy right here," Turtle nods to the owner.

The burly owner unlocks the glass case and retrieves a black .357 Ruger revolver. He rests the gun on the counter. Turtle gestures RoRo to pick up the revolver.

"She's a pretty one, RoRo. Go 'head. See how she feels," Turtle edges.

RoRo grips the pistol and aims it at one of the mounted deer heads high up on the wall. As Turtle stands next to him observing his every move, RoRo pretends to enjoy the moment.

"Six hun'erd wit' papers. Eight hun'erd – no papers," the owner injects.

RoRo was an intelligent student who took a wrong turn and things got worst when he hooked up with Turtle a few years ago, but at times, his intelligence resurfaces. Something the shop owner said isn't adding up right to RoRo. Wearing a confident expression, RoRo whispers into Turtle's ear, reminding him of how most street dogs back in DC usually went into neighboring Virginia cities such as Arlington and Fairfax to easily get whatever firearms they wanted. Turtle nods agreeably then coolly looks at the shop owner.

"State law here says there ain't no license required for handguns so ain't no papers needed anyway, but hey, I ain't mad at ya' though 'cause we all gotta lit'l hustle in us," Turtle preaches.

Feeling a little guilty and desperate to make a sale, the owner spits out another price, "Tell ya' what y'all, gimme five hun'erd an' I'll throw in a box of bullets – no charge."

Being a bit of a show-off, Turtle begins to slowly peel off hundred dollar bills from the thick bundle in his hand then lays them atop the counter.

"One..two..three..four..five," Turtle counts, briefly pauses then coolly begins to peel off a few more hundreds and places them atop the small pile already there, "Six..seven..eight. Extra two for stayin' open for us – one mo' for a separate box of .44 caliber bullets. See, told ya' I'd make it worth yo' while. And look at that, you still got yo' eight – papers or no papers."

Happily, the burly gathers up the eight bills, stuffs them into his shirt pocket then bends down to retrieve the boxes of bullets from the glass case.

Turtle turns to RoRo as he grips the black revolver.

"Now that the vice president is properly armed, he can help me take this fuckin' town," Turtle boasts.

RoRo responds with a half-hearted nod.

❧

 Minutes later, Turtle's Escalade is parked in the lot of Serv City Inn. Angie is in the front passenger seat facing Turtle. RoRo is in the backseat listening to Angie going over details.

"Gimme ten minutes. I'll call or text the room number," Angie affirms.

"Do whatcha do, baby," Turtle nods.

Angie steps out and heads toward the lobby entrance door.

Inside the lobby at the registration desk, the night clerk is handing a room key to a horny trucker standing next to a scantily-clad prostitute. Angie enters. The trucker turns around. He freezes. He's stunned by Angie's tantalizing body and movie star good looks. Teasingly, the trucker's companion gives him a jealous look then slaps his shoulder.

Next to the registration desk, a larger poster-size sign propped on an easel advertises the upcoming TALENT SHOW in the adlacent lounge. Angie looks around rapidly. Her head angles in every direction then abruptly stops with a satisfied nod as her eyes fall upon the Ladies Restroom several feet away. Angie steps in front of the registration desk.

"Is Carl here?" she asks.

The desk clerk politely responds, "He should be right –"

Coming from the left corridor, Carl suddenly appears behind Angie.

"And there he is," the clerk points.

Carl places his hand on Angie's shoulder.

"Looking for me?" he asks.

Putting on her bedroom eyes, Angie slowly turns around in a suggestive manner and softly asks, "Can we go somewhere private an' discuss what we'd talked about?"

Carl nods to the desk clerk, "Hand me the key to one-o-four."

The clerk retrieves the key to room 104 from the sizeable key board behind him then hands it to his boss.

"Carl, I'm gonna go to the ladies' room. I'll meet you in the room," Angie injects then teases him with a flirtatious wink as she steps away.

Behind the closed door of the ladies' room, Angie quickly pulls her cellphone from her waist clip then calls Turtle.

"Room one-o-four," Angie says then hastily puts her phone away.

In room 104, Carl is sitting on the edge of the bed anxiously anticipating Angie's entrance. Seconds later, Angie steps in. She shuts the door behind her but slyly ensures that the knob stays unlocked.

"Won'tcha com'on over here an' let me getta taste of 'em sweet nipples," Carl says while licking his lips.

Stalling for time, Angie very slowly sways her hips then begins to take off her blouse. She seductively peels off her left sleeve then…BAM! The door swings open!

Turtle and RoRo burst into the room brandishing their guns! Pulling up her left sleeve, Angie quickly backs away from Carl as his eyes widen in surprise. The barrels of Turtle's .44 Magnum and RoRo's new Ruger .357 are mere inches from Carl's nose.

Carl blurts, "What the –"

"Shut yo' country ass up!" Turtle cuts in.

Carl glances at Angie. He senses that she knows the two intruders.

"You set me up?" Carl sighs.

Turtle tightens his grip on his Magnum as the barrel kisses Carl's nose. Fear invades Carl's redden face.

"My girl tells me ' you the big man 'round here, Carl. Hey, look here, Carl, they call me Turtle an' I'm yo' new business partner. From now on when the girls pull a trick make sure I get my ten percent so we don't have to go through that change of management shit. I'll be here once a week to pick up my cut. You think you might have a problem wit' that, Carl?" Turtle asks while shoving the barrel harder against Carl's nostril.

Nervously, Carl shakes his head 'no.'

Turtle removes his gun out of Carl's face then tucks it under his waistband. Following Turtle's lead, RoRo returns his revolver as well.

Turtle extends his hand for a shake and offers, "Carl, my man, I look forward to doin' business wit' ya."

Reluctantly, Carl shakes Turtle's hand while shooting Angie a dirty look.

"We ready to bounce or what? This room stinks," Angie interjects.

"Alright, let's go visit this wine lady," Turtle says then looks directly at Carl and asks, "Whatcha know 'bout this lady in Spotsylvania who makes wine from flowers, dandelions or some shit like that?"

Carl's taken aback, "Who? Sweet Ma'Raine?" he asks.

"Where ' she live?" Turtle nods.

Protectively, Carl questions, "Why? She don't bother nobody. You ain't got –"

Swiftly, Turtle snatches his Magnum from his waistband then whips it hard against Carl's face! SMACK! Carl's portly body tumbles to the floor.

"Carl, my man, if we ' gonna be business partners, you need to be more helpful, not all difficult an' shit. So, my man, do you know where this Ma'Raine lady lives?" Turtle reinerates with a sinister grin.

On the floor wiping the blood from his busted lip, Carl struggles to speak, "Out on Route Five. It's that two-lane road that runs all –"

"Hey that's the road we live on," RoRo interjects.

Angie shakes her head in disbelief then softly mumbles, "So stupid. ' Should leave his stupid ass."

Turtle hears Angie's sly remark. He steps toward her with a menacing gaze!

"Say it again, bitch! Go 'head! Say it again! You ain't goin' nowhere 'til you pay me whatcha owe me! You know how many times I saved yo' ho ass, bitch! You owe me! You ain't goin' nowhere!" Turtle barks!

"Com'on, Turtle. Let's just go, man. She ain't mean it, man," RoRo pleads.

"Don't fuck wit' me, Angie!" Turtle snarls again!

Turtle sighs then decides to take RoRo's advice. He begins to walk towards the door. RoRo and Angie follows him out of the room as Carl wipes the oozing blood from his now swollen lip.

Chapter Fourteen

Pattys Blood

Patty is sitting alone at her kitchen table drowning herself with her mother's homemade wine. There's a small amount left in the tall bottle position next to a sizeable pile of losing lottery scratch-offs. Already a little woozy, Patty grabs the neck of the bottle and sucks down the last drops. Speaking to herself with a slurred tongue, she begins to rehearse for a visit with her mother, something she has purposely avoided for several years, "Mama, I'm sorry I ain't visited you. Maybe we can talk an' spend some time together like real people do. Jesse's gonna be leavin' soon. You ' all I got now, Mama. All I got."

Half drunk, Patty struggles to stand then staggers to the nearby counter and snatches her car keys.

Beaming rays from Ma'Raine's porchlight reflects off of the spinning twenty-two inch rims on Turtle's Escalade pulling up in the front yard. Turtle eases the front bumper up near the leaning porch. RoRo, Angie and Turtle steps out then make their way up the porch steps to the screen door. There are pronounce bulges in RoRo's and Turtle's shirt tails as they try to conceal their hardware under their waistbands. RoRo lightly brushes up against the screen door and, to his surprise, it moves.

"It's open," RoRo softly utters.

Turtle opens the door further as they all step onto the slanted porch. Angie, RoRo and Turtle make faces and glance at one another in response to the COUNTRY MUSIC they faintly hear coming through an open window. Since the screen door was left open, Turtle nonchalantly checks the doorknob on the door leading into the house. He twists the knob and to his surprise, the door opens.

"See, that's the good thing 'bout these country people, they don't be lockin' their doors," Turtle says with a sarcastic grin.

Following Turtle's lead, RoRo and Angie casually walks into the living room. The country music is much clearer now as it bellows from a radio in the adjacent kitchen. Following behind Turtle, Angie and RoRo calmly walks across the living room towards the kitchen.

Ma'Raine is sitting at the kitchen table labeling bottles of her homemade dandelion wine. She peels off a self-adhesive label from one of the sheets Jesse had printed out earlier then proudly sticks it on the tall bottle of wine. She places the finished bottle aside then labels the next bottle.

The radio atop the refrigerator continually fills the air with vintage country classics. Casually, Turtle, RoRo and Angie enters the kitchen. Totally focused on the task at hand, Ma'Raine is unaware of their presence as she methodically label the bottles. Turtle walks over to the refrigerator, reaches above and turns off the radio. Startled, Ma'Raine nearly falls out of her chair!

"Who? – Now that's just plain down right rude! Just plain rude!" Ma'Raine angrily protests.

Turtle, RoRo and Angie circle around the kitchen table directly in front of Ma'Raine. Full of fire and old-fashioned Southern guts, Ma'Raine has no fear in her face. Genuinely astonished by Ma'Raine's confidence and audacious demeanor, Turtle tries to take control of the moment and save face in front of his two young sidekicks.

"Rude? I'll show ya' rude, bitch!" Turtle boasts as he hastily grasps one of the wine bottles on the kitchen table and hurls it across the room! BAM! The bottle crashes against the sink counter! Pieces of glass splatter across the floor!

Ma'Raine fiercely holds her own, "I ain't 'fraid of you or ya' friends. Who ' y'all anyway? And why ya' come in my house actin' like that? Ain'tcha got some type of manners? Damn dogs act better than that!"

Ma'Raine's mentioning of 'dogs' hits a nerve in Turtle. The very thing that he's trying to distance himself from has just been thrown back into his face. Turtle snarls at Ma'Raine then whips out his gun from his waistband! He shoves the barrel of the cold Magnum hard against her wrinkled face!

Turtle glances at one of the generic labels on the wine bottles then growls, "Listen, old lady, I'm Turtle an' I'm the new co-owner of Ma'Raine's Dandelion Wine. And let me tell you how I operate. Everytime you sell a bottle of that good ol' dandelion wine you ' gonna make sure I get ten percent an—"

Boldly, Ma'Raine shoves the cold barrel of Turtle's Magnum out of her face and abruptly burst into LAUGHTER!

Taken aback, Turtle, Angie and RoRo glance at one another with peculiar faces as feisty Ma'Raine fires off, "Co-owner? Ten percent? Yeah, y'all must be the new folks who just moved here. Now let me tell y'all some'em an' y'all listen to me real good. You can try to dress like us, talk like us, eat like us, but you – an' I ain't talkin' 'bout black an' white now – but you ain't never ever gonna be one of us! You can't just come to a quiet little place like Spotsylvania an' act like that. People like you can never be like us. You ain't us! Young man, we FIND our place in this world – we don't FORCE our way in it! Even 'em dandelion wishes know that! Hell, they float an' float for miles hoping they might get lucky an' find a place to root."

Defiantly, Ma'Raine chuckles then utters, "Co-owner, ten percent – must be crazy."

Turtle has heard enough! Enraged, he whips Ma'Raine across the face with the butt of his gun! SMACK! She tumbles to the floor groaning in pain! Towering over her, Turtle barks, "Look, grandma, don't fuck wit' me! I hope you know that them damn flowers you be pickin' be coming outta MY fields! Yea, you heard me right. I just bought all 'em fields 'round here and you can either cut me in on yo' lit'l country moonshine hustle an' we work together like a happy family in peace or I can bust yo' old ass for trespassing on MY fuckin' land!"

Meanwhile, out in the front yard, a weaving Toyota Camry pulls up behind the luxurious Escalade. Patty steps out. She staggers as she makes her way alongside the flashy Cadillac. Looking hard at the gleaming SUV with curious eyes, Patty mumbles to herself, "Hm, I guess even rich folks likes Mama's wine. Hm, I knew it was good but I ain't think it was that damn good. Hm."

Patty wobbles toward the porch steps.

Back inside the kitchen, Turtle is standing over Ma'Raine with his arm drawn back, ready to strike and pistol-whip her again. Already in tremendous pain, Ma'Raine throws her hand up to block Turtle's blow when Patty suddenly enters! Out of her mother's view and quite tipsy, Patty looks at Turtle, Angie and RoRo with drunken eyes. Unaware of her injured mother on the floor, Patty drunkingly stutters, "Y'all like my mama's wine t—"

Ma'Raine finds the strength to pull herself up off of the floor and tries to warn her daughter, "Patty, get outta –"

Turtle backslaps Ma'Raine with the side of his gun! SMACK! Ma'Raine crumbles to the floor again.

"Mama?" Patty calls out as she frantically staggers across the kitchen to her mother's side. Blood begins to trickle from Ma'Raine's swollen lip as Turtle towers over her and her drunken daughter with ominous eyes.

"Like I was tellin' yo' mom, I want ten percent from each bottle sold. I'll be comin' around once a week an' somebody betta be handin' me some cash," Turtle reinerates as Patty shakes her head in disbelief.

"Mama ain't got that kinda money. She just makes 'nuff to keep this place goin'. She ain't makin' no big profit. She ' just doin' some'em she likes," Patty pleads while comforting her groaning mother.

RoRo looks at Ma'Raine's bleeding lip and sighs. He doesn't like what Turtle is doing. RoRo is anxious. He wants to leave but is too afraid to speak up. Somehow he summons the courage and nervously suggests, "Turtle, man, maybe we should just go. I think they got the message."

Turtle is certainly not one to be told what to do. Angie already knows that all too well, and now RoRo is going to get schooled on that fact. Turtle walks up to RoRo, nearly nose to nose.

"Aw, look at this now. Lit'l runaway nigga thinks he can man up to me now! You tellin' me what to do now, RoRo? Who the fuck's runnin' this shit? You RoRo? Who?" Turtle angrily questions!

Submissively, RoRo lowers his head and softly answers, "You."

Immediately, Turtle steps back from RoRo then faces Patty and Ma'Raine with a gentler approach, "Look, I'm a nice guy once you learn to get along wit' me. And all I'm sayin' is –"

Patty maybe drunk but she easily reads Turtle's bullshit and she's had enough. She boldly interrupts and defiantly gives him a piece of her mind, "Fuck you, bitch! You ain't nuddin' butta bitch if ya' hit a lady this age. You need a gun 'cause you ' too weak to be a real man! You ain't nuddin' butta little BITCH!"

Stunned, Turtle freezes then quickly thinks about how to handle this. Turtle's plans aren't always well-thoughtout. The silence is stretching. Angie looks at RoRo. Donning a blank expression, RoRo looks at Angie. They both know that you can't disrespect Turtle in that manner and not pay a price.

Turning to Angie, Turtle orders, "Baby, won'tcha take this drunk outside for a minute."

Patty throws her arms over her mother's shoulders. She doesn't want to leave her mother's side. Concerned, Angie bends down to speak to Patty. Angie whispers, "It's better to do what he says. He ain't playin' wit'cha."

Patty glances at Turtle towering over her with a piercing gaze. Reluctantly, Patty stands and is lead out of the kitchen by Angie. Whatever Turtle is planning, he's keeping the details to himself as he slyly orchestrates a reason to keep Ma'Raine and RoRo inside the house. Turtle looks at Ma'Raine whimpering on the floor then nods to RoRo, "Help this lady an' get her cleaned up."

Turtle casually walks over to the refrigerator, reaches on top and turns on the radio as a country classic loudly fills the air. RoRo walks over to Ma'Raine. He gently picks her up off of the floor and helps her into the nearest chair at the kitchen table. Unbeknownst to RoRo, Turtle leaves with a tight grasp on his .44 Magnum. RoRo goes to the sink. He rinses out a dish cloth. The kitchen is permeated with country music and the sound of running water.

Outside in the front yard, at point blank range,Turtle aims his Magnum at Patty's head. Hysterically, Patty pleads for her life. Angie sees no mercy in Turtle's eyes so she turns her head and shuts her eyes. POW! Tiny blood droplets sprinkle the back of Angie's neck. She shivers. Patty deflates to the ground alongside her Toyota Camry.

Back inside, at the kitchen table, RoRo wipes Ma'Raine's bloody lip with the dampen cloth as another country classic echoes from the radio. RoRo and Ma'Raine are oblivious to the activity outside. The running water and radio had completely drowned out the gunshot. Angie walks in and signals RoRo that it's time to leave. RoRo follows Angie out of the kitchen. Ma'Raine's face contorts in pain as her head tilts back then quickly jerks forward.

She fights to keep her eyelids open then gradually passes out at the kitchen table.

In the front yard, Turtle sits behind the wheel of Patty's Toyota Camry. Strapped in the seatbelt, Patty's body is propped up in the passenger seat. Turtle pokes his head out of the window as RoRo and Angie steps off the porch steps. Momentarily, RoRo stiffens as he is hit with the realization of Patty's outcome.

"Follow me!" Turtle hollers out the window.

RoRo and Angie hops into the Escalade. RoRo's behind the wheel. He glances at Angie with a peculiar look. The kind of look a caged animal has that wants to escape but don't know how. Angie sighs agreeably. Turtle backs the Camry out of the yard. RoRo backs up the Escalade then follows Turtle down the two-lane blacktop.

Underneath the bridge that connects Spotsylvania County to the outskirts of Fredericksburg, Patty's Toyota Camry is parked near the river's edge. The front bumper is facing the Rappahannock's slow-moving water. The driverside door is open. Turtle is repositioning Patty's body from the passenger side into the driverseat. RoRo is standing near the rear of the Camry waiting for Turtle. Angie is sitting in the Escalade parked on a low-lying dirt road a short distance away. The Escalade's headlights illuminate the shady activity taking place at the river bank. Turtle slams the driverside door then walks back to the rear of the car to join RoRo. Together, Turtle and RoRo pushes the Camry over the edge and into the deep, murky waters of the mighty Rappahannock. Turtle stands at the river's edge watching the Toyota get swallowed by the river. Satisfied that all evidence has been submerged, Turtle nods then gestures RoRo to follow him back to the Escalade.

Chapter Fifteen

Ro

No one has seen LaBrea since she'd left Ma'Raine's house on her bike. As the dark sky looms above, there's a desperate search for her throughout Spotsylvania and Fredericksburg.

Standing in the doorway of a brick home on Courthouse Road, LaBrea's father Sheriff Woods is showing a photo to a woman wearing pajamas. The lady shakes her head 'no.'

In a vast open field, two Sheriff deputies and a group of volunteers brandish flashlights as they comb through high weeds and patches of wild flowers, thoroughly inspecting every inch with each step.

At Katie's Burger World, Jesse's blue '77 Nova is parked amidst other cool-looking, souped-up hot rods outside of Fredericksburg's most popular teen hangout. After receiving their food at the pickup window, the spirited teenagers go to sit at the numerous patio tables encircling the bustling joint. Balanced on his customized crutches, Lamar is showing a picture of his sister to a table of teenage girls. One by one, each girl shakes her head 'no.' A few feet away, Jesse is speaking to another group of teens and showing them a photo of his girlfriend LaBrea. All of them shake their heads 'no.'

஌

At the edge of the forest near the single-lane blacktop, LaBrea is desperately clinging to life. She slowly crawls out of the dense woods. Badly bruised and swollen, she reaches the soft shoulder of the quiet road. Her clothes are tattered and blood-stained. It's dark. No traffic. LaBrea is breathing hard as she inches along the edge of the road.

Moments later, bright beaming headlights illuminate the blacktop! Frantically, LaBrea musters all of her energy to crawl towards the center of the road. Approximately fifty yards away, traveling at regular speed, a pickup truck is making its way down the backcountry lane. In the middle of the road, LaBrea tries to yell out something but nothing comes out of her moistureless. Trying to raise her bruised right arm, she groans in pain as her arm lifts barely an inch. Suddenly, the moving pickup brakes and screeches to a stop a few feet from LaBrea! Mister Henry, a local farmer, jumps out of the truck.

"Hey! You ' alright?" Mister Henry asks.

LaBrea is unresponsive. Mister Henry hurries back to the pickup and opens the passenger side door. He rushes back to LaBrea and carefully lifts her off of the road.

Gently, he places her in the passenger seat, buckles the seatbelt then shuts the door.

Minutes later, Mister Henry's pickup speedily swerves into the half-circle driveway of Rappahannock General then hastily stops in front of the Emergency entrance.

On a lonesome dirt road, Sheriff Woods is driving his cruiser at a snail's pace, twisting his neck looking in every direction as he passes by sporadic patches of woods and farm fields. It's been a long night. The Sheriff is weary as he urgently searches for his missing daughter.

Suddenly, the Sheriff's two-way radio alerts a BEEP! One of the deputies back at the station speaks, "Woody, come in. Woody, come in."

"This is Woody. Go 'head."

"Woody, your daughter's at Rappahannock General."

"Thank you Jesus!" the Sheriff sighs while making a wild U-turn then floors the gas back down the desolate road!

It's getting late. Jesse's Nova is parked along the left guard rail of the bridge above the Rappahannock. There's no traffic. The tranquil sound of trickling water is filling the air. Under a moonlit sky, Jesse and Lamar are leaning against the guard rail gazing down at the slow-moving river. Lamar's crutches are propped against the rail next to him. Looking dog-tired, Jesse sighs, "Where could she be?"

Reassuringly, Lamar nods, "Ww..we'll ff..find her."

Abruptly, Lamar's cellphone rings. As fast as possible, he digs it out.

"Hello," Lamar quickly answers.

As Lamar listens, his face illuminates with joy. Jesse is anxious to hear the news.

"Oo..okay, Dad," Lamar says while turning to Jesse.

"Sh..she's at th..the hos..hospital," he utters while tucking his phone away without hesitation, Jesse runs to the car and hops behind the wheel! Hurriedly, Lamar grabs his crutches and manages his way back into the passenger seat! Jesse makes a crazy U-turn then floors it across the bridge to Fredericksburg!

During this time of the night, things are normally pretty quiet in the Intensive Care Unit. In LaBrea's room there's a constant beeping sound from the heart rate and blood pressure monitors along with oxygen and thermometers surrounding her bed. LaBrea's face is nearly covered with bandages as she lies in bed with tubes protruding out of her mouth and right nostril. An intravenous line slowly drips saline solution from a hanging bag into her vein on her left arm. A series of thin colorful wires with adhesive leads are attached to her forehead and other parts of her battered body, connecting to the electronic meters and digital monitors displaying constant changes in her vital signs.

Sheriff Woods is standing alongside the bed holding LaBrea's fingertips.

"We're gonna get whoever done this to you, sugar. I promise you," the Sheriff utters with strong conviction then lowers himself to kiss his daughter's fingers, "I love ya', sweetheart."

The Sheriff turns to leave and is met by Jesse and Lamar entering the room.

"What happened?" Jesse anxiously asks.

"We don't know yet but somebody worked her over pretty bad ," the Sheriff sighs, struggles to spit out the words, "And she was raped."

The news stuns Lamar and Jesse. Sheriff Woods leaves the room with a look of vengeance. Jesse and Lamar steps alongside LaBrea's bed. Jesse touches LaBrea's fingers as a lone tear trickles down his cheek. Lamar runs his hand along the top of the blanket covering her shoulders.

With a harden look of determination in his eyes, Lamar utters, "LaBrea, I'm gg..gonna mm..make 'em pp..pay."

"LaBrea, this is Jesse. Can you hear me?" he asks. There's no response.

"LaBrea, who did this to you?" Jesse continues.

Seemingly at first, there's no response and then suddenly LaBrea's fingers on her right hand begins to rapidly move as if she's trying to tell Jesse something.

"You want something? You need something? The nurse?" Jesse asks.

LaBrea gestures and moves her right hand in a writing motion as if she was holding a pen.

"Ss..she ww..wants tt..to ww..write ss.. some'em," Lamar injects as Jesse dashes out of the room! Moments later, Jesse returns with a pen and pad. He gently places the pen between LaBrea's fingers then holds the pad firmly in place. LaBrea slowly begins to scribble two alphabets on the pad. Two awkwardly drawn letters spell out 'RO' on the pad. Lamar and Jesse are intensely looking at the scratchy letters, trying to figure out their meaning.

"Ro?" Lamar utters.

"Ro?" Jesse thinks hard for a moment and then it hits him, "RoRo? Roland?"

LaBrea repeatedly taps the pen on the pad, signaling 'yes' to Jesse. Instantly, Jesse drops the notepad and without a word goodbye he flies out of the room!

Lamar takes the pen from his sister's fingers then gently places her hand into his.

Chapter Sixteen

Pattys Body

Jesse's blue Nova pulls up in the driveway. A thousand thoughts are racing through his mind as he steps out with a baffled look. He notices that his mother's Toyota Camry isn't parked in the driveway. Patty is normally home at this late hour. Jesse goes inside and checks the kitchen. On top of the kitchen table is an empty bottle of Ma'Raine's Dandelion Wine and a big pile of losing lottery scratch-offs.

"Mama? Mama?" Jesse calls out.

There's no answer. Jesse's puzzled and concerned about his mother's whereabouts but other matters are consuming him now as he hastily migrates toward his bedroom down the hallway. Jesse enters his room and quickly grabs the neck of his Martin guitar propped in the corner. Got what he'd came for, Jesse dashes out with his prized guitar in tow.

Three hours later, the morning sun is beginning to break through the parting clouds. Fredericksburg is still asleep and Jesse's Nova is the only vehicle parked on Caroline Street in front of a pawn shop. Stretched out in the front seat, Jesse is sleeps. His pricey Martin six-string rests on the backseat.

Near the bridge, two fishermen are out early this morning on the Rappahannock. They are on a small aluminum boat in the middle of the slow-flowing river. One of them gets excited as his fishing line is suddenly pulled tight. The fisherman reels the line but it's not budging. His hook and line is submerged near the left bank.

"There's some'em in the water ov' there."

"We betta check it out."

The fishermen maneuvers the boat towards the left bank.

"Holy shit!"

The fishermen spots the roof of a car just below the surface of the water. Immediately, one of the men pulls out his cellphone and calls the authorities.

A short time later, an army of Spotsylvania County Sheriff deputies, Fredericksburg police officers and paramedics have convened near the river bank as a heavy-duty tow truck pulls the Toyota Camry out of the water. Sheriff Woods is on the scene. As the Camry is pulled up on the river bank, the Sheriff and a few others shake their heads in disbelief as Patty Raine's bloated body becomes visible strapped behind the wheel.

Chapter Seventeen

The Bus

Back in town at the Caroline Street pawn shop, Jesse is at the counter trying to negotiate a fair price for his Martin guitar. The shop owner is thoroughly looking over the immaculate six-string.

"I can take it for three hundred," the owner offers.

"That's a six hundred dollar baby there an' you know it!" Jesse claims.

"Four hundred. Take it or leave it," the owner firmly says.

Jesse's cellphone abruptly rings. Reluctantly, Jesse nods 'okay' as the shop owner begins to place bills atop the counter.

"Hello," Jesse answers his phone.

Instantly, a solemn look covers Jesse's face. He'd just gotten the heartbreaking news about his mother Patty. Jesse sighs then quickly tries to gather himself. Minute by minute, Jesse's world is falling apart. He focuses on the mission he'd initially started. He scoops the money off of the counter then hurriedly leaves the shop.

Jesse's blue Nova speeds across the bridge to Spotsylvania. Below, on the left bank, emergency response vehicles, police officers, the County Coroner's van and a handful of local news reporters are still on the scene. Jesse sticks to his mission. He glances out the window at the activity below but he doesn't slow down. Jesse's out for vengeance and nothing's stopping him!

At a rundown trailer park tucked away off of Sullivan Road in the county, Jesse pays a quick visit to a well known hustler who can get you anything you need for the right price. Jesse stands in the doorway of a rust-spotted mobile home as a slender, bearded man with suspicious eyes hands him a sawed-off shotgun and a box of shotgun shells. Jesse hands the man a wad of bills then hastily dash away back to his idling Nova.

While most of the Spotsylvania County deputies are down by the river bank,

two of the Sheriff deputies are at the station trying to find out who exactly are the real people hiding behind the aliases Turtle, RoRo and Angie. One of the deputies is on the phone and jotting down notes. The other deputy is at the computer clicking and looking back and forth between a gallery of mug shots and shared data files among law enforcement agencies.

Hanging up the phone, the deputy is elated with the information he'd just got wind of, "Hey, get this, the one calling himself Turtle is really Winston Nelson Niles.

The girl Angie is really Cynthia Bates and the boy RoRo is actually Roland Campbell."

Immediately, the other deputy on the computer types in the threesome's real names. Suddenly, the monitor flashes 'MATCH! MATCH!MATCH!' and the printer starts spitting out a continuous roll of past criminal activity, helpful background details, current warrants and updates.

The deputy who was the phone is scanning the lengthy printout.

"These ain't no angels, that's for sure," the deputy comments.

Scanning various reports on the screen, one in particular catches his colleague's eye, "Check this out, a beat detective in DC says the word on the street there is that Turtle had stole a ton load of cash from a drug deal and now these DC punks are on their way here to get their money back and take Turtle out."

"We better get Woody out there before there's a world war three here in lit'l Spotsy."

A taxi travels down Plank Road then pulls into the yard of Johnny's Salvage And Sales. The taxi parks in front of the garage where Raul, the mechanic, is working on the underbelly of an old Buick. Lamar's listless left leg protrudes from the rear door then the bottom of his crutches soon follows. Grasping a stuffed envelope, Lamar struggles out of the backseat as the driver keeps the engine running idle. The look on Lamar's face is the same as Jesse's, the look of vengeance!

Lamar maneuvers his crutches toward the garage as his left leg dangles freely. With each step, Lamar glances at the antiquated school buses for sale. Raul wipes his greasy hands off with the rag dangling along his pants leg then steps out to greet Lamar in his usual broken English, "Hey, my friend."

Lamar's in a hurry. Right away, he hands Raul the thick envelope, "Th..that's tt..two th..thousand ff..for the bb..bus."

"Yes. You happy. Me happy. Me boss Johnny happy too," Raul nods.

"Can you dd..do mm..me ' ff..favor?" Lamar asks.

Lamar maneuvers back near the buses. He wants to show Raul something.

"Yes, me help you. No problem," Raul says while joining Lamar near the two buses.

Raul points to the bus that he and Jennifer had discussed, "That ' one for you."

"Cc..can you tt..take off dd..door?" Lamar asks.

"No need door?" Raul asks with a puzzled face.

"No nn..need dd..door," Lamar reinerates.

"No problem, me friend. You no like door, I take door off. Me fix anything. You like me clean for you too. I clean. No charge. No problem," Raul nods.

Lamar shakes his head 'no' then repeats, "Just tt..take off dd..door an' pp..please cc..ccheck bb..battery. I nn..need gg..good bb..battery."

Raul nods 'okay.' Satisfied, Lamar hurriedly maneuvers back to the awaiting taxi. Lamar moves surprisingly fast as his crutches maintains quite a steady pace.

"I cc..come bb..back!" Lamar shouts back to Raul.

"You come back and bus ready for you, me friend," Raul responds as Lamar gets into the backseat of the taxi.

Minutes later, the taxi pulls up curbside at 613 Caroline Street, one of Lamar's favorite places, Harrison's Hobby Shop. Lamar gets out of the cab. Again, the driver waits, leaving the engine running as Lamar works his way into the store.

Mister Harrison is placing a new shipment of model car kits on the shelf. Lamar enters. It's obvious to Mister Harrison that Lamar's not his usual self.

"Mornin', Lamar. Is everything alright this mornin'?"

Lamar doesn't have time for their usual chitchat. He digs out a folded piece of paper from his pants pocket then hands it to Mister Harrison.

"Hey, Mister Har..Harrison. Cc..can I gg..get th.. these items?" Lamar asks.

The two of them have been friends for years but Lamar's anxious demeanor this morning has got Mister Harrison stratching his head as he unfolds the piece of paper.

"Hm. Looks like a big project," Mister Harrison remarks as he quickly scans Lamar's shopping list then makes a face.

"Yup. A bb..big one," Lamar nods with a serious expression.

Mister Harrison grabs a hand shopping basket then starts down the first aisle. He studies the list again then retrieves several packs of BB's. He goes to another aisle and retrieves numerous containers of play dough, packages of silly putty and a large roll of aluminum foil. At another aisle, he places various rocket-style fireworks and numerous sleeves of firecrackers into the basket. The basket is full. Mister Harrison goes upfront and places the basket next to Lamar standing at the counter. Lamar quickly scans the contents of the basket then nods pleasingly as

The Bus

Mister Harrison retrieves another basket and continues down another aisle where he picks up two rolls of duct tape, two spools of thin electrical wire, a can of motor oil and two remote-control units normally used for R-C model aircrafts and R-C scaled vehicles.

Across the bridge in Spotsylvania, the newcomers have awaken to a different sun this morning.

RoRo is sitting on the edge of his bed. He's deep in thought. Angie walks in.

"Can I talk to you for a minute, RoRo?"

RoRo scoots over a little. Angie plants herself beside him.

"I'm thinking about leavin'. Soon as I get some money I'm gone," Angie sighs.

"Yeah, I been thinkin' about that too. I ain't down wit' all this killin' an' shit," RoRo adds.

In the living room, Turtle is drinking a cup of coffee. He hears the roaring sound of an car engine. He migrates toward the window and eases back the edge of the curtain. Jesse's '77 Nova is pulling up in the driveway behind Turtle's Escalade.

"RoRo! Angie! We got company!" Turtle alarms.

Angie and RoRo joins Turtle in the living room. Turtle gestures RoRo to look out the window.

"You know that fool?" Turtle asks RoRo.

Peeping out the window, RoRo sees Jesse marching towards the front door brandishing a sawed-off shotgun!

"That's Jesse. He's gotta gun an' he means business!" RoRo alarms.

Turtle immediately unlocks the front door then hides behind it.

"Tell me when he's at the door," Turtle orders RoRo.

RoRo moves the curtain slightly again as Angie smartly steps aside, out of the projected line of fire.

"He's close!" RoRo alerts.

Turtle places his hand around the doorknob as RoRo lifts a finger, signaling Turtle to get ready. Seconds later, RoRo's raised finger suddenly dips! Right on cue, Turtle swings the door open! The door rams Jesse head-on! BAM! Jesse stumbles backwards and hits the ground hard! Turtle easily takes the sawed-off shotgun from Jesse's loosen fingers then aims the shorten barrel at his head!

"Get up, motherfucker!" Turtle snarls.

Jesse struggles up then is forced inside as the barrel pokes the middle of his back. While stepping into the living room, Jesse abruptly crashes to the floor as the butt of the shotgun swipes the back of his head! Turtle slams the door shut then turns around and hurls his right shoe hard into Jesse's ribs!

Unbeknownst to Turtle, Sheriff Woods' cruiser and two accompanying deputy patrol cars arrive in the front yard. Fully geared up in bullet-proof vests and protective wear, one of the deputies goes around to the rear of the house as the Sheriff and his other deputy examine the SCRATCH MARKS running alongside the luxurious Cadillac Escalade.

"Looks like hunters' scratches to me, Woody. Right near where Mister Henry said he found your daughter. Ain't nuddin' but sticks 'round there an' you don't get scratches like these not unless ya' goin' through a path like that. We got our man alright," the deputy nods.

Moments later, the deputy who'd went around the back suddenly returns with LaBrea's bicycle. He walks the bike next to the Sheriff's cruiser.

Sheriff Woods sighs, "That's hers," then adds,"We're gonna need more backup here. Get Fredericksburg on the radio. See if they can send some cars out here."

The Sheriff reaches into his cruiser and retrieves his megaphone. While glancing up he takes a longer look at the blue '77 Nova then mouths 'Jesse' while shaking his head.

Using his vehicle as a shield, Sheriff Woods speaks through the megaphone, "Winston Niles! Cynthia Bates! Roland Campbell! We know who you are and if Jesse's in there, you gotta let 'em go. You don't wanna make things any worse. Y'all done wore out yo' welcome and it's time to com'on out now."

Abruptly, the front door opens. Jesse is tossed out into the yard like a bag of garbage. He's unconscious. His listless body rolls a few feet then stops.

One of the deputies makes his way across the yard as the Sheriff covers him with his high-powered rifle. The deputy grips Jesse's ankles and drags him out of harm's way near the parked cruisers further out in the yard.

"He's hurt!" the deputy alarms.

Sheriff Woods turns to his other deputy, "Get the paramedics out here!"

Seconds later, several Fredericksburg Police cruisers arrive. This is fast becoming a massive standoff. The sound of SHATTERING GLASS echo through the air! The front window of the house is being busted out! The sawed-off shotgun taken from Jesse is protruding from the shattered window! POW! POW! Pellets fly everywhere! Everyone takes cover behind the parked vehicles!

☙❧

Across the bridge, at Johnny's Salvage And Sales, reinforcement is covertly underway. Although Lamar wasn't interested in having the school bus washed, Raul, having no clue to what the old scraggily vehicle will be transformed into, is cleaning the dirt off the sides with a bucket of soapy water. As Lamar requested, the door has been removed. Lamar is on the bus completing the first phase of his mission. His military expertise as a demolition specialist in Iraq is being utilized here as he combines generic everyday materials to plan and conduct his sophisticated operation. Lamar is forming modified C-4 bombs with a mixture of motor oil, play dough, silly putty, BB's, and gun powder taken from the fireworks and firecrackers he'd purchased at the hobby shop. Methodically, Lamar uses the silly putty and play dough to shape softball-size explosives, wraps each ball with aluminum foil then places them randomly on the seats. Each foiled ball has two electrical wires protruding from it. The thin wires run along the floor in the middle of the aisle towards the front of the bus. Upfront, strategically within arm-reach of the driverseat, two modified detonators, made from the remote control units, are duct taped to the instrument panel. One series of wires are bundled and connected into one of the homemade detonators, as another series of wires are bundled together and runs underneath the instrument panel apparently towards the battery.

❡❡

Back across the river on the county two-lane, a convoy of three fast-moving Hummers is headed straight towards Turtle's house. Each Hummer is stuffed with meaty, mean-looking street dogs. The Hummers' license plates all show 'District of

Columbia.' Barrels from AK-47's begin to poke out of the Hummers' windows as they fast approach the line of Sheriff deputies and city cops positioned in front of the house.

POW! POW! POW! Shots are fired from the AK-47's to clear the path towards the house. The rapid-fire bullets got the out-gunned deputies and city officers running for cover! The three Hummers burst through the line of cops and stops in the middle of the yard! The menacing thugs jump out of the Hummers as an oncoming, speeding school bus steals everybody's attention! Lamar's behind the wheel and he's aiming directly towards the house!

Lamar briefly shuts his eyes for a quick prayer then reopens them as he nears the front yard. He keeps his left hand steady on the wheel as his right hand reaches toward the instrument panel. His fingers are an inch away from the taped detonators! Methodically, just like he'd planned it out in his head, Lamar flicks the joysticks on his makeshift detonators then hastily springs from the driverseat and leaps out of the fast-moving bus!

The unmanned, speeding bus RAMS into the Hummers! BAM! CRASH! Still going, the bus burst through the living room of the house! BAM! CRASH! Then, suddenly a resounding explosion! BOOM! BOOM! BOOM! The bus and entire house goes up in flames as bellowing smoke and flying debris fills the air! The mob of DC thugs, Turtle, Angie and RoRo are drowned in clouds of dirty smoke as they all scatter and try to escape across the yard. Immediately, a swarm of Spotsylvania deputies and assisting Fredericksburg officers tackle and handcuff each one of them as they cough up the nasty smoke. One by one, the harden thugs from Washington, Turtle, Angie and RoRo are led to the backseat of awaiting cruisers.

Near the rear wheel of Jesse's blue Nova, Lamar is flat on the ground groaning in pain from his hard, tumbling landing. Then, amidst all of the melee and chaos around him, Lamar notices that something truly miraculous has happened. His left leg begins to move! Excitedly, he moves it again! And one more time, he works his left knee and repeatedly rotates his left foot, "Mmm…my leg! Mm..my ff.. foot! Look! It's mm..moving!"

Chapter Eighteen

Changin Face

Several days later, in the back of a small church, Miss Taylor, Bunny Smith and a group of friends from Spotsylvania High are giving their condolences to Jesse who is standing remarkably cowboy strong in spite of his family's loss and the profound shiner and abrasions under his eyes. Grasping a bountiful bouquet of fresh-cut yellow dandelions, Ma'Raine weeps as she kneels next to her daughter's grave. Standing beside Ma'Raine and still partially wrapped in bandages, LaBrea places her hand upon Ma'Raine's shoulder as Ma'Raine tosses the bouquet of dandelions atop Patty's coffin.

A few feet away, Lamar is standing proudly WITHOUT his customized forearm crutches. Surrounded by a group of admirers from the church,

Lamar is finally feeling like a real hero as he tells the group how he rigged the old school bus with modified C-4 explosives and gives an explanation of his miracle, "Mmm..must ff..finally gg..got that nn.. nerve sss..stim..stimulation ee..electric cc..charge mm..my therapist always ss..said I nn..needed, I gg.. guess."

Everyone nods agreeably then a gentleman steps forward and says, "Lamar, your girlfriend Jennifer told us about that other school bus for sale over at Johnny's and we're gonna take up a donation here at the church next Sunday and get that old bus for you so you can get started on your shuttle business."

LaBrea slowly turns around and looks for Jesse. Something is weighing heavy on her heart as she shuffles her way towards him. She gently guides him away from the group of mourners, easing herself closer to him. She looks at him with somewhat shameful eyes and softly asks, "Are we gonna be okay, Jesse? Maybe we shouldn't see each –"

"Hey, how can I have Jesla if we breakup? I don't have time to be thinkin' of another name if I married a Brenda or a Donna. What I'm gonna name my daughter then? Jesbren? Jesdon? No way. I like Jesla," Jesse quips.

"Boy, you ' just plain country crazy," LaBrea teases then melts into Jesse's chest as he reassuringly throws his loving arms around her.

A few nights later, the Serv City Inn is hosting their highly anticipated talent contest. The lounge is crowded with truckers, travelers, lot lizards and many locals showing their support for the handful of homegrown performers. As a young man with a guitar steps off the platform to a lukewarm applause, Jesse takes the stage. Feeling somewhat naked in the spotlight, Jesse is without his prized Martin six-string. Jesse winks and nods at familiar faces sitting in the audience. LaBrea is sitting next to Ma'Raine. Lamar is sitting between his father Sheriff Woods on his right and his girlfriend Jennifer Day on his left. As Jesse adjusts the mike stand on stage, Jennifer glances at Lamar with a bit of sparkle in her eyes.

Jesse begins to speak into the microphone, "Hi y'all doin'? I don't have my guitar but –"

From the audience, the busboy who works in the restaurant across the street, graciously hands Jesse his guitar.

"Thank you," Jesse nods to the boy then continues to introduce himself, "My name's Jesse Raine an' I like to sing a new song I wrote."

Jesse begins to strum the guitar strings. He fine tunes a couple of the strings while speaking to the attentive crowd, "This song's about leavin' an' wantin' to leave. It's called Changin' Face."

Jesse strums the guitar to a soft, melodic rhythm and begins to sing...

> Here we go.........changin' face
> Just like the river....in the race

Here we go…..changin' face
Just like the dandelions….in the wind
Feels like blood……getting' thin
Here we go……changin' face
Just like the river…..in the race
Maybe these dreams of ours….just floats away
Here we go again……changin' face
Just like dandelions…..in the wind

-To Be Continued -

Acknowledgement

Song lyrics to "CHANGIN' FACE" were written by Randolph Randy Camp

*Writers Guild of America, East Reg. Number: R25183, October 2008

*US Copyright Office Reg. Number: PAu 3-414-222, October 2008

About the Author

Randolph Randy Camp was born on March 12, 1961 in rural Spotsylvania County, Virginia. As a child, Randy began to use his strong imagination to escape his sometimes dismal surroundings. As he got older, Randy absolutely loved going to school. He developed a love for creating colorful characters, storytelling, writing poems and short stories throughout his school years. Randy graduated with Honors from Spotsylvania Sr. High School in June 1979. Later, during the summer of 1979, Randy enlisted into the US Air Force and begin to travel the globe going from base to base. While stationed at Kadena Air Force Base on the Okinawa Islands Japan, Randy attended the Overseas Division of University of Maryland University College during his off-duty hours. After leaving the military, Randy began to devote more time to his writing career. In 2007, Randy was a Winner of the Quarter-Finals Prize at the Writers Network 14th Annual Screenplay & Fiction Competition in Los Angeles, California. Two of Randolph Randy Camp's favorite quotes are "Don't let others define you – You define yourself!" and "Don't be afraid to dream Big!"

Other Books by Randolph Randy Camp

- Then The Rain: A Contemporary Rock n' Roll Thriller
- Wet Matches: A Novel

Made in the
USA
Monee, IL